MERCY'S RISE

GUILD OF ASSASSINS: BOOK THREE

LACEY CARTER ANDERSEN

Copyright 2022
Published by Lacey Carter Andersen
Cover art and design by Enchanting Covers
Editing by Rainlyt Editing

This work of fiction is intended for mature audiences only. All characters are over the age of eighteen. Names, characters, places, and incidents are either a product of the author's imagination or are used fictitiously. Any resemblance to any persons, living or dead, business establishments, events, or locales is entirely coincidental.

This book is protected under the copyright laws of the United States of America. Any reproduction or other unauthorized use of the material or artwork herein is prohibited without the express written permission of the author.

DEDICATION

To my cat, Pumpkin— You have been with me for many wonderful years. Seeing you be such a comfort to my kids always reminds me about how incredible you are, and how lucky we are to have you.

1

Mercy

I'd lost too much time when the damned tire blew out on my stolen car. You'd think the *mighty* vampire king would have more reliable vehicles.

"Damn vampires," I mutter to myself, but my words come out tense rather than sarcastic.

But the delay doesn't matter: I'm back on the road, and the miles are flying past. By nightfall, I should reach the guild. I just hope it'll be soon enough to save my father, Tasha, and the other living guild members.

I'd tried calling Tasha back since her cryptic call begging for my help, but she hadn't picked up. And each time I called and got sent to voicemail, my anxiety increased. I just can't picture a logical scenario in which my father, a prisoner to The Shadow League, and Tasha would be at the guild together. A scenario where most of the members are dead and the others are being held. The only thing I have concluded is that The Shadow League is waiting for something.

I just hope it isn't for me. *Because of what I am.*

A shiver rolls down my spine as images from the book on rare creatures flash through my mind. Of the phoenixes, beings all other supernaturals believe are extinct. *Except my father and I are still alive.*

I can recall in perfect clarity the picture in the book of the woman strapped to a chair, a prisoner, used for her blood, so that others could drink it and become immortal. *If I'm being lured into a similar situation, what will I do?*

I never thought I'd be desperate enough to take my own life. But knowing that I'm the only one who can permanently kill myself without being reborn if I tear out my own heart...well, it changes things. It changes the hard line I imagined I had. Because such a thing might sound extreme, and yet, if it's the only escape from a lifetime of torture, I can't completely rule it out.

Which is horrifying.

Music blares on the stereo. A new song. I hadn't even realized it was playing. I turn it down, but then right back up. I don't want to be alone with my dark thoughts, not about my dad and Tasha. Not about my future. And not about the three men I left behind, leaving no trace that I was there except a note. I know they'll be mad when they open it, but I can't drag them into more trouble, no matter how much I appreciate the fact that I know they would willingly have my back in this situation. Hell, in all situations.

Because I have to do this alone. This crazy, stupid thing, all to save a man I've never known. A man who could even be lying about being my biological father.

My gaze shifts to the rearview mirror. I'm practically flying down this quiet highway road. There have been very few cars on it over the past couple of hours, and those I'd seen, I'd easily sped around and left behind. So to see a car actually gaining on me makes me take notice. *What the actual fuck?* The car has to be edging close to a hundred miles an hour. I'm desperate, but not *that* desperate to get to my location. That speed is going to kill someone.

"Idiot," I mumble, then tell my middle finger to stay right where it is.

The car's on my ass within moments. It's a red four-door sports car with tinted windows. I wave for it to go around me, but the jerk doesn't. Instead, he hugs my ass so hard I almost want to yell for the guy to buy me dinner first, and then he jerks into the lane beside me and the driver rolls down the passenger's window.

There, I see a very pissed-off Rian glaring at me from behind the steering wheel. I'd gotten under the vampire's skin a thousand times already, but even I feel like this is a *whole* other level. His gaze alone burns through me, and he indicates that I need to pull over with angry gestures that might as well just be his middle finger. I see Bash in the passenger seat. His arms are crossed over his chest and his lip is curled, but he doesn't look in my direction.

Well, fuck. I guess I'm in trouble.

I pull over, heart racing. My whole plan fades away in the blink of an eye. I've come up with every possible scenario about how I will break into the guild and save the people I care about without being hurt. Nowhere in any of my plans are these three idiots (because I'm sure Ares is in the backseat) stopping me from reaching my destination.

Not that I'll actually *let* them stop me. This will be nothing but a delay.

I turn off my engine as they stop not far in front of my car, and I get out, my legs aching as I stretch them. The guys are out of their car in an instant, slamming the doors closed and storming toward me. Bash is the leader of their little pissed-off group, and I actually have to hold back a laugh as

I spot him. There are few things the guy cares about more than his appearance, but it's clear he didn't spend a second getting ready. His blond hair is an absolute mess, and he has circles under those pale green eyes of his. His green shirt is wrinkled, as are his jeans, and the laces on his boots haven't even been done.

"What the ever-loving hell?" he shouts toward me.

I lean against the hood of my stolen car and cross my arms over my chest. *This is going to be fun.*

Rian is behind him, right on his heel. The vampire doesn't have the same angry little march going on. His anger is quieter. A prince's anger. The anger of a snake waiting to strike. His light brown hair, always a little long and disheveled, looks fucking sexy. His beard, always neatly trimmed, has a little bit of wildness to it. And instead of wearing one of his formal button-up shirts, he has a grey t-shirt on that seems too tight, hugging the big muscles he so often seems to want to hide. His dark eyes meet mine, and he lifts a brow that says more than Bash's angry question ever could.

"Nice to see you, fellas," I call.

Ares is moving toward me more slowly, but he gives me a disappointed look after I greet them. And damn it, his disappointment feels worse than the other two's anger. Like if I had a parent who actually cared about me and I did something to upset them. He has sunglasses pushing back his black hair and bruises that have mostly faded from when we were attacked by his pack. Lucky bastard. Sure, I can die and come back to life all peachy and perfect, but until then, I still have all the injuries from our fight with the pack, and they are definitely going to slow me down a little, which I don't appreciate one bit.

Bash is suddenly there. He grabs me and shakes me by

the shoulders, his expression wild, and I'm a little shocked. "What do you think you're doing? Huh?"

"Driving," I tell him, because I never do know when to shut up.

He looks like he wants to hit me, but instead, he drags me into his arms and holds me so tightly that I actually have to gasp, "Air."

Instantly, he releases me, but he looks like he wants to hug me again. "*Had to go*? What the fuck kind of note is that?"

"A purposely unhelpful one," Rian says behind him, and his glare deepens.

He's right, so all I do is shrug. "How did you figure out where I was anyway?"

"GPS." Rian practically grits out the word.

Oh, right. Technology. The bane of my existence.

"So where are you going?" Ares asks, and I can't read his tone. He's not even looking at me anymore, just staring down at his feet.

"We brought you to Rian's for a reason, or did you forget?" Bash grits out. "It's the only place we can keep you safe from the hellhounds, from the people who know what you are and are hunting you, now that you've been kicked out of the guild. Going on some wild road trip is going to get you fucking killed."

"Don't worry, I won't stay dead for long," I tell him, trying to sound chipper.

Given his glare, I'm thinking that was the wrong thing to say.

"It seems you're on a path straight back to the guild." Rian isn't asking, just stating. "A guild you were kicked out of."

I glance at Ares, hoping he'll help me out, but he's still

staring down at his shoes, his expression upset. Betrayed, even.

Sighing, I say, "Look, it's not like I'm going somewhere to have a quick fuck or something. I got a call. A call I needed to take care of. *By myself*."

"The second you fucked us, you stopped getting to just take care of things yourself," Rian states.

"I haven't fucked Bash!" Oh boy, that clearly wasn't the thing to say, given the sharp looks all three of them give me, so I try again. "Besides, I'm sure you all have slept with women and then not become joined at their hips."

Crickets. *Damn it. Did I say the wrong thing again?*

Bash looks at Ares. "Say something before I strangle her!"

The shy wolf glances from him to me, and then he hesitantly moves closer to me, and I feel the walls I've so carefully erected around my heart start to crumble. "Mercy, where are you going and why? I know you're used to doing things on your own, but after all we've done, after all we've sacrificed, don't we at least deserve to know that?"

He's not...wrong, but I'm not either. "If I told you guys, you'd want to come with me."

"We're coming with you either way." And Ares just sounds so damned sure of himself that it gets to me a little.

"I'm walking right into the fire on this one."

"You're always walking straight into a fire, and for some reason, we're always following right behind you," he points out, his tone gentle, which is hard to argue with because that does seem to be our MO.

I release a slow breath, sure I'm making a mistake before I even start talking. "Tasha called me. She said the guild was attacked, most of them were dead, and some of them were being held prisoner, including my father."

"You mean the mysterious man who turns to ash who claims to be your father?" Bash asks, followed by a snort.

"He is my father!"

"You wanting a father who actually gives a shit about you doesn't mean you should just accept the word of a stranger claiming to have the title," Bash says, glaring.

"Fuck you!" I whirl away from them and storm toward my car, heading back to the driver's side.

Rian is there in an instant, using his freaky vampire speed against me to keep my door closed. "Nope, you're not just going to leave now."

I flash a smile at him. "Try to stop me and I'll put my dagger through your dick."

I try to open my door, and he slams it shut.

"Rian!" I spin to face him and poke him in the chest. "This has nothing to do with you."

He catches my hand, yanks me against him, and kisses me. But it's not a little kiss. It's not a kiss to calm me down. He's sending a message. A message that I belong to him. And the message is definitely received.

His mouth is hard and cruel. Punishing my own. Forcing me to spread my lips so that his tongue can dart inside, which sends heat racing straight to my core. He captures me between his body and my car, then grabs my ass, pressing me against his erection. My head begins to spin, and I lose all logical thoughts. If he tried right now, I'm pretty sure I'd fuck him right here.

Instead, he breaks our kiss, runs his lips down my throat, and then bites me lightly, his fangs sliding into my throat.

I gasp as more pleasure rolls through me, and I wrap my hand in his hair as he feeds on me. My hips rock against his erection, and he groans before pulling back. He's panting, eyes wild as he stares down at me. "Try that again, and I'll keep you chained to my bed."

"Promise?"

He grabs my breast and rubs my nipple through the tight leather. "Promise." But it sounds more like a threat.

Ares clears his throat, and I shove Rian away, remembering where we are and why. Then, I turn on the other two. "Do you see now why I wanted to do this myself? I'm running straight into danger, and I know it. But I'm doing it anyway. And I know it's not logical. And I know you all think I'm stupid for it. But I'm doing it no matter what. And there's nothing you can do to stop me."

Bash and Ares exchange one of their looks, the one where I feel like they're sharing a million thoughts without a single word, and then Bash turns back to me. "I guess we're going to be stupid too because we're going with you."

I frown. "No, it's too dangerous."

Bash laughs. "Come on, Mercy. We know you well enough to know we aren't going to talk you out of this. Look at us. Do you think we're going to let you go alone?"

The answer comes easily. "No."

"So let's get your stuff and get it in our car. It's time to do something stupid."

And there must be something wrong with me because Bash has never been hotter.

Damn it. I'm a mess.

2

Mercy

It's nearly dark when we start on the narrow dirt road that leads to the guild. It curves through the woods, where everything around us is eerily silent. Or maybe it's only eerie because I know at the end of this road death and danger waits for us. Rian is driving, because I guess whatever stupid car we're in is expensive and has a lot of power, and having a vampire with quick reflexes driving at fast speeds seemed smarter than having me do it. At least according to the guys.

Like they have a clue.

"It's going to be okay."

I glance back. Ares and Bash are comically smashed into the back seat, but they'd insisted I take the front seat. It was oddly gentlemanly of Bash, but exactly what I would have expected from Ares.

"I know," I tell Ares, trying to sound casual.

He gives me that look, the one that feels like he's staring into my very soul. "It really is."

I glance away. I don't need Ares looking into my soul right now and seeing all the cracks, because then I have to look at them too. The cracks that say maybe I *am* being stupid. That maybe I am diving into danger for a man I don't even know. But my heart wants to believe he's my father, and that he needs me to save him.

That he needs me for *something*.

The people who raised me never needed me for anything. Yes, Beauty and her beast wanted me to play the part of the beautiful daughter, of their princess and heir. But now that they have my brother, they don't even need me for that anymore. Something they've made abundantly clear. But I'm not just rushing into danger to soothe the ache in my heart, I'm doing it because I can't...*not* do it. As stupid as it might be that I want to become an assassin to protect people, it's true. I want to protect Tasha, my father, and the others, whether it's the right thing to do or not.

"We just need to be smart about this," Bash says, using that voice that drives me crazy. The one that implies I'm *not* going to be smart about things, even though he's not *necessarily* wrong.

"I'm always smart."

I can feel Bash's gaze burning into my back. "We saw that The Shadow League has a whole force behind them. We won't win head-on. We need to sneak in, get a sense for what's going on, sneak back out, and form a plan."

"A plan," I repeat, unable to stop the snort that slips out.

"Mercy, be serious," Rian says, all regal vampire prince-like.

I roll my eyes, then realize my foot is bouncing and force it to stop. "I am. I get it. Okay? You guys haven't exactly been subtle on this drive that you think this is a bad idea and that you're worried I'm going to go in without a thought and just get myself killed."

"Damn, and we were trying so hard to be subtle," Bash mumbles.

I turn around and glare at him. "If you don't want to follow my crazy ass into this fight--"

"I'd follow your tight ass into any fight," he tells me, and there's amusement in his eyes. "No matter how crazy you are."

For Bash, that's sweet.

Rian pulls over onto the side of the road and eases into the trees. He turns the engine off, and our car is suddenly way too quiet. None of us moves. None of us gets out of the car. Finally, Rian says, "We should walk the rest of the way so they don't see us coming." He's stating the obvious, but it's better than the silence.

"And remember that we can only do what we can do," Ares says, his voice barely above a whisper. "Sometimes we have to make hard choices."

I understand what he's saying. Rubbing the sweat on my palms onto my pants, I keep my voice as steady as I can. "For real, if there's no chance we can save them, I'll accept it. I won't get you all killed."

"Don't make any promises you can't keep," Bash says, then opens his door.

Damn it. I hate his arrogance, but he's right. There's a reason I rarely make promises. The second I get in a situation I tend to act without thinking. But I swear I'm going to try my hardest to keep my men safe. They gave up their spots at the guild, as well as their own safety, countless times for me. The least I can do is to protect them too.

We all get out of the car, and then the guys go to the back and shove my stuff in the trunk around to pull out the weapons hidden underneath. They get themselves equipped with anything they think they might need. I don't follow them, because I don't need any more weapons. I place the sword that was in the passenger seat next to me on the hilt on my back. Then I double-check my two magical daggers and the other little weapons hidden around my body. It only takes a second, and afterwards I watch them strapping themselves up, and I find myself staring. It's oddly sexy to see my wolf, vampire, and not-quite-human Bash getting ready for a fight.

Having men who are murderous is quite the turn-on for me it seems. I should probably talk to a therapist about that someday.

Bash's gaze meets mine. "See something you like?" *Damn it, it's lame, but it's hot.*

"Yeah," I tell him in a sultry tone. "Those blades are well made, aren't they? Probably sharp as hell and well balanced?"

He shakes his head at me, but he's smiling.

Then, the trunk is closed quietly and the tension changes between us all. I know Rian isn't an assassin. He hasn't spent his life training for this job the way we have, so I'm surprised by how seamlessly he seems to pick up on the change. We all move without speaking a word, slipping deeper into the woods, but still close enough to keep an eye on the road. We travel like that for a while, until we can see the fence and the gates of the guild.

Instantly, we're all kneeling down, and my gaze slides over it all, trying to figure out every small detail. First, the most obvious things. Some motherfucker had knocked down the gates. Gates that have stood for longer than I've been alive, gates enchanted with expensive spells and guarded by dangerous supernaturals. They hang half off the hinges, blackened as if they'd been struck by a ball of fire. Or something equally powerful. The walls in various places are also black and burned, probably where we had lookouts. And sure enough, when I let my gaze move to the ground, I see charred shapes that can only be bodies.

Damn it. Our enemies are sick bastards. Sick bastards who would torture my father, one of the last phoenixes in existence, probably using him for his damn blood to remain immortal, and then go and attack a bunch of young adults. Yeah, we're training to be assassins, and we're not exactly innocent, but we also don't just go into people's homes and slaughter everyone. These people are starting a war, and I don't understand why.

Maybe I'll know more soon though.

There's only one way in since none of us can just fly over the wall. Technically, Bash can teleport short distances, but it requires a lot of his energy and is pointless if the rest of us have to walk through the open gates. So, we slide toward the open gate, ready for anything, but find no signs of our enemies. Still, I go first when I don't see any danger, rushing across the lawn under the darkening light of evening and slipping behind a tree, heart pounding. My men come in behind me, and then we're all kneeling, watching once more.

Waiting for trouble.

But again, I sense nothing. *See* nothing.

I look at my men. I've come to realize that some of the senses I always thought were normal might have been because I'm not as human as I thought I was. But all my men have refined senses, as supernaturals themselves, so I want to see if any of them have noticed anything. A scent. A sound. Anything at all.

But after a moment, they shake their heads.

That should probably make me feel better, but it doesn't. I close my eyes and slowly steady my breathing, letting my senses stretch out. Sometimes this works. I don't completely understand it, but it makes me feel like I'm aware of things that my normal senses can't pick up on. And sometimes doing this does nothing. This time, I get the strangest feeling. An awareness of people in the dining hall, but nowhere else. I search deeper, but I can't be sure. It's like I'm looking at my world, just underwater.

I open my eyes. "The dining hall."

They nod.

"The spy point," Bash says, followed by another nod from Ares and Rian.

Uh, what? "Spy point?"

"There's a place where we can see into the dining hall without being seen, but getting there might be tricky," Ares explains, then kneels down and draws a rough map in the dirt. It's getting dark and hard to see, but I get the general points. He stands and we all look at the guild once more.

As much as I want to dive right in and attack these assholes head-on, I gave my word. What's more, that plan is stupid. Not that I like agreeing to someone else's plan, but I do it. I follow Bash as he leads us a back way through the main guild building I'd never even known existed. We take stairs concealed behind a wall. And even though I try to remember exactly the winding, weaving path we take through halls and up more stairs, I feel a bit turned around by the time we stop at another door.

Ares gestures for us all to be quiet, not that we need to be told. But still, my heart is racing, and when I realize that, I know I'm already screwing up. Depending on the types of supernaturals we'll be fighting against, they could hear my heartbeat if I don't control it better. So, I close my eyes and take several slow, deep breaths. I practice what I've done a thousand times before, then open my eyes, knowing my pulse has slowed, quieted, to a point that most supernaturals would never be able to detect my presence.

And from the looks on the faces of my guys, they've done the same.

Bash moves to the wall and slowly pushes against it. Ares moves to his other side, and they shove until there's a small space just big enough for us all to move through.

They indicate for me to let them go first, and I nod, even though I don't like it. I've never been up here. It only makes sense that they go in front of me. But this is my fight. I'm the reason we're here, and I'll be damned if I let any of them get hurt for my choice.

So the second they go through, I slip in after them, ignoring the irritated look my prince gives. Yes, I know he's stronger and faster than I am, but hell, that doesn't make him a better fighter or a better assassin, and what we're doing requires stealth.

On the other side of the wall is a small balcony that feels high up even before I inch next to Ares and Bash and carefully look down. But, sure enough, we're above the dining hall. And below us?

My gut twists. Tasha and the other assassins-in-training and admins are across the stage. Their hands are bound behind their backs, and their ankles are bound too. All of them have been beaten severely, to the point where I don't recognize many of their faces. And blood continues to drip off of them in slow drops, falling on the already blood-coated floor. Around them are men and women in black clothes with black cloaks. I don't recognize them either, but they're clearly with The Shadow League, the group that attacked the guild before. The group that was holding my father prisoner.

But the man in question is nowhere to be seen.

I do a quick count of the people scattered around the room. Since this seems to be the location of the main battle, there are bodies everywhere; at least fifty of them. As for the living, there are about two dozen of our people and an equal number of theirs. Between the four of us, we might be able to take them down, depending on what kinds of supernaturals they are, but definitely going in guns blazing could get one or more of us hurt or even killed. Something...different is needed in this situation. I'm just not sure what.

But my thoughts are spinning.

Rian gestures for us to step back into the hall, and we all silently obey. We move further from the opening to the dining hall, so we won't be heard, and in a low voice, Rian says, "What's the plan?"

No one answers and my spinning thoughts begin to take shape. "I think I have an idea, but it's a little crazy."

Bash grins. "We wouldn't expect anything different."

He's right, but this is crazy, even for me.

"Who wants to see me die?"

3

Mercy

This is so damn stupid, I hope it's smart. I stand in front of the big doors leading into the dining hall, take a deep breath, and then throw them open. "You wanted me, fuckers; here I am!"

All eyes turn to me. Friend and foe alike. My daggers are in my hands already, and I throw one without a thought. It hits one of my enemies square in the head, and he's falling before any of them have so much as breathed. I throw the other one only a second later, and it goes through the throat of a woman, who crumbles to the ground. I whisper the magical words, and my daggers fly back into my hands.

"Come on, bitches, what are you waiting for?"

And I see it hit them, see the raw fury that comes over their faces, and I plant my feet more firmly on the ground, knowing what's coming next.

They rush me, but there's something uncertain about their movements. I push forward, running straight at them, then freeze right before I crash into the first opponent. Locking eyes with him, I spin my daggers around myself, not giving them any direction that they can attack without tasting one of my blades. They slow, closing in around me from all directions. And then, I force a smile that is so at odds with everything I feel and slit my own throat.

Death closes in on me, but now I know what to expect.

Or do I?

I expected pain. I expected to die and be reborn with my injuries from the last fight gone. I even expected the fire that blasts from my body, frying the people to death as they scream around me. The book had said with each death a phoenix would come back faster, more powerful, and with the fires of the phoenix around them, so it was new, but not startling.

But the massive fiery wings that explode out from my back and lift me right off the ground, leaving the bodies surrounding me behind? *That's* a surprise.

For a minute, I'm wobbling in the air, not sure how to control them. I feel awkward as I go too high one moment then seem to be falling the next, before catching myself at the last second. It's scary, and a bit strange. But I have to quickly push past the fact that I have wings and focus on learning to use them before I become a liability. I start to flap my wings slowly, evenly, and I gradually level out. Which just feels...right. Like I was always meant to have wings.

Feeling confident, I take a deep breath and launch across the room with my daggers in hand as everyone stares at me in shock. The dozen or so remaining enemies barely have time to react, when my blade takes out another one of them, and another one.

My men race into the room with a howl and a snarl, and then they're fighting the others. Swords clang against swords. Claws and teeth tear into flesh.

Bash uses his demonic powers to appear behind his enemies and slice off their heads. Rian's sword and fangs work, almost in unison. His sword strikes down opponents and his claws and fangs injure anyone who gets past his blade. Ares has shifted into a wolf, and he leaps, attacks, and moves with lightning-fast reflexes. Together, they look like they're fighting completely inexperienced civilians rather than the warriors that seemed to have taken down most of the guild members.

Which is weird.

But when they're done, no one is left standing except us.

Ares transforms once more from the wolf with black fur and brilliant green eyes into a man. He rises, wearing nothing but torn threads of his earlier clothes. Rian wipes the blood from his mouth and hands, then glares around the room. Bash's sword and hands are covered in blood that he seems to completely ignore.

I land lightly on the ground, and the wings behind me fade away. Rushing to Tasha, I cut away the rope binding her mouth and the words come exploding from my lips. "Where's my father? Is he okay?"

She looks at me in confusion. "Your father?"

"Mercy." His voice makes every muscle in my body tense.

I stand to my full height and turn toward the open doors. He's there, my father. His body is dark, made of nothing but ash, and his eyes are burning red. "Stop this."

"Stop what? I'm here to help you. To save you from our enemies." I'm moving toward him, heart in my throat.

He cocks his head and lifts his hand to point at Tasha and the others on their knees. "*They* are our enemies. They are the beginning of the end of the phoenixes."

"What? No." *What in the hell is he saying?*

Suddenly, some of the burnt bodies on the floor near me

begin to move. The creepy blackened figures shake like zombies awakening in a horror movie. Ash rises and swirls around them as they seem to piece back together and swell. Bash hauls me back from them, shifting me towards Rian and Ares until we're all gathered together with our backs against the wall. Six of our enemies sit up, alive once more. Blackened ash falls off of them until they seem entirely untouched by the fire, and my horror-filled gaze snaps to my father.

"*They* are your people. They're half-breeds, but phoenix blood runs through their veins just like ours. They are here to exact our revenge. To get justice for all that has been taken from us. We will never be safe until every last one of our enemies dies."

I'm shaking my head. "No, a bunch of young people are not our enemies. They have nothing to do with what happened to the phoenixes."

He smiles. At least I think he's smiling. "They have *everything* to do with it. They're assassins to the great families. The same families that destroyed our kind. Once they are gone, the families will be vulnerable, and we will finally be free."

"No." I don't know what to say, but I feel oddly scared and confused as more of the dead bodies littered around the room begin to twitch and move. "This isn't right."

The enemies around us are beginning to stand, to reach for their weapons. In seconds, we'll be in trouble again, and my whole 'killing them all in my own death fireball' thing probably won't work again. My men and I could all end up dead, along with the people we came here to save.

But I can't let that happen. Even if my father isn't the innocent victim I'd imagined he was.

Leaping forward, I slice the binds on Tamara's wrists and

ankles, then move to the next person. My men see what I'm doing and do the same. "Get up!" I shout to the injured students and faculty. We're yanking them to their feet, away from the awakening phoenixes. "If you want to live, get up and fight!"

My father begins to blow away like ash on a windy day. "Stop this, Mercy. You are one of *us*. Not them. There is so much you don't understand."

"I won't stop! I won't let you kill them!" I tell him, still frantically freeing more assassins.

A man, who had been dead only moments before, shouts, "What do you want us to do about her?"

The top of my father's head is gone, and his eyes are falling away too, but his mouth moves. "Leave them for now. Give her more time. But before long, she *will* join us."

And then the rest of him blows away, leaving nothing but ash drifting in an unseen breeze.

The phoenixes eye us with anger, but they move toward the door, never turning their backs on us before they disappear out into the hall.

I collapse onto my knees. *My father is the leader of this murderous group? He commanded this slaughter?*

"Mercy..." Ares kneels beside me.

But all I can do is shake my head. Whatever this is, whatever just happened, I don't understand it. Or maybe I'm not ready to. Not yet.

4

Bash

I can't believe Mercy's insane plan worked...sort of. I find it a lot more believable that the creepy ash man is a bad guy. Looking over at Mercy, I tap my foot on the ground, then lean back against the wall of the infirmary. She's looking after Tasha, even though there's nothing she can do about it. Only one witch survived the massacre, and she's in no shape to heal people, so everyone has just been scrambling around, using whatever potions and spells are available to heal the injured. Tasha has been wounded, but as a strong shifter, she'll be okay.

Still, I know this is how Mercy is with the people she cares about. She keeps them at arm's length, never tries to show her vulnerable side, but would also give her heart and soul to protect them. She's weird like that. Lovable and annoying as hell.

At last, she gives Tasha a little smile and pushes away from her bed. Her gaze locks with mine, and her false smile falls away. She doesn't even slow as she passes me, but she knows she doesn't have to. I'm going to follow her. Following her is one thing I've always been good at.

I'm practically her shadow as I move through the hall. She doesn't glance back at me, but it's clear from her stride that she knows I'm behind her. She leaves the main building, then takes the stairs of the tower that make up the human dorm with a casual stride. When she reaches the door to her room at the top, she types a code into the panel beside her door and it clicks open. She enters, then spins around and stares at me, one brow raised.

"What are we doing?" I finally ask her.

I see it in her eyes. She doesn't have a clue. But she'd never actually admit it. "Right now, we're seeing to the injured."

"And after that?"

She hesitates, and then those small hands of hers curl into fists. "Then, I'm going to figure out the truth."

"What truth?"

"If the guild was responsible for what happened to the phoenixes, and how much of a hand the most powerful supernatural families had in all of this."

I sigh.

"What?" Her question is an accusation.

"I just think it's a waste of time. All of this. Those people, whether they have reason to hate us or not, killed and injured a bunch of people. They're insane. And it sounds like their only goal is to cause more death and destruction. We should be reaching out to the families, telling them to increase their security, and asking them to lend us warriors to take down that group."

Those big blue eyes of hers flash with some unnamed emotion. Maybe surprise. Or hurt. "You just want to kill all of them, including my father, without even trying to understand their motivation?"

"I don't need to understand their motivation other than that it's fueled by revenge. Revenge serves no purpose. At the end of it, you're just left empty. Trust me, I know."

She moves a little closer to me, and some of her cockiness falls away. "People know what I am now, Bash. So where can I be safe?"

I stiffen. "With us. You'll always be safe with us."

"What? Hidden behind spells at the guild or in Rian's mansion?"

"For now."

"For how long?"

"I don't know." My words come out more frustrated than they had in my head. "But this is our best option. Keep you somewhere safe. Destroy our enemies. And then figure it all out."

"And you say I'm rash," she accuses.

"You are. I'm not. This is just the smartest thing. We can't give them more time to get ahead of our defenses. We have to figure out a way to protect ourselves and our people."

"Your people," she says softly.

"Mercy..."

"What?" Her gaze catches and holds mine. "What makes these people mine? The fact that I know some of them? That I grew up with some of them? I don't belong here; they've made that clear. No one even wanted me here."

"And yet you risked your life to save them."

She's quiet, which isn't like her at all. And then she says, "Yeah, I couldn't let them die, but that doesn't make them my people. I'm not saying I want to join the phoenixes on this mission, but I'm also not saying they're my enemies."

I shake my head, wishing I could shake her. "What do

you want to do, Mercy? Because you know we're with you, every step of the way."

She goes to her bed and sits on the edge, looking lost. I hesitate, then follow her, sitting beside her. To my surprise, her head falls on my shoulder, and she gives a deep sigh. "Maybe I don't completely know yet."

I can't help myself; I smile. "That's okay too."

"We do need to warn the families though. I just wish we knew which families they planned to attack."

And then it hits me. The solution to both our problems. "The archives. The hidden ones. Everything that the guild knows is there. If they have any involvement with the phoenixes, we can figure out what it is, and we can figure out which families were involved. At least then we can have a clearer picture of what's going on. And until then, we can just contact all the families, so they can be on their guard."

Her response isn't enthusiastic, but she says, "Okay."

"Mercy?"

She slowly looks up at me, and her expression is so damned lost.

I touch her face gently. "We're going to figure this out. I promise."

"I know. But why does it feel like I'm betraying the only family I ever really had by taking any step at all?" Her voice is as lost as her expression.

I lean forward and kiss her lightly on the cheek. "You're not. You're just not going into this thing blindly." And then I say something I probably shouldn't have. "Once upon a time you blindly gave your loyalty to a family that never gave it back. That was okay, but we have to learn not to make the same mistakes, and I'm telling you, you could easily slip into the same thing with this father of yours."

She nods as if coming to some conclusion. "You're right. I don't like that you're right, but you are."

"No finer words have ever been spoken."

She gives a little laugh that makes my heart feel warm and punches me lightly in the arm. "Shut up."

"I will if you will."

And as she shakes her head, I know we're going to be okay. At least, I hope we will be.

5

Mercy

Out of all the people that could have survived, seeing that Master Snatte was among the living wasn't exactly something for me to be excited about. And yet, when I asked her about learning the guild's secrets, she seemed almost eager to take me into the forbidden place where their secrets were kept. It was such a contrast from the chilly way she had interacted with me since coming here that I almost thought it was a trap, but Ares reassured me that having a near-death experience and knowing a bunch of creatures who couldn't be killed wanted her dead was the real reason behind her change in attitude. So I tried to make peace with it when she agreed to take me to search for information about my father and the phoenixes.

Bash and Rian stayed behind, contacting the families of the deceased to tell them about who was lost, and also to warn all the great families that danger might be coming for them. I wished they didn't have to tell them about the phoenixes, but they do. The only thing they held back was that my true father might be their leader, and for that I was grateful.

"It's right this way," Master Snatte says, checking back to see that Ares and I are still following her.

We are, of course—where else would we be—but Ares gives her a reassuring nod. He might be awkward, but he's kinder than I am. I only manage to give her a half-irritated look as she takes us to the library. A library we already know about. But I hold my tongue, because like all old manors, every room tends to have secrets, and I would bet she isn't going to just take us to a random shelf in the library that contains forbidden knowledge about the guild.

Sure enough, she leads us to a back corner and slides a dusty book out. We spot a keypad hidden behind it. She types in a code and I pretend not to notice the keys she hits, but I memorize the damn thing, and then watch as she swings out the whole bookcase, revealing a door behind it. She types in yet another code beside the door, and it pops open, revealing a dark staircase.

To my surprise, she lights a torch in a sconce by the stairs and hands it to me, then looks at Ares. "All our most important books will be found below. The ones you're looking for are on the last row of shelves at the very bottom in the right-hand corner. I'm not sure which of the books will contain the information you're looking for, but that's where our most shameful secrets tend to be kept. And if we had any involvement in the destruction of the phoenixes, that would be something we wouldn't want known."

"Because all the many people we've killed aren't shameful," I say.

She pushes glasses up her nose, and I see a small crack in one corner as she leans closer. "Mercy, our responsibility is to train assassins here. Not because we want a lot of people in the shadows slaughtering one another, but because the people trained here protect the powerful. They protect our system. Our rulers. The heirs. They kill when they have to, but that's to be expected. Participating in the genocide of the phoenixes is not something that's expected. Not in this time or in any other would a group want to be involved with such a thing. It's horrifying, to say the least."

I know she's right. I'm just being pissy, for whatever reason.

"Okay, I guess we'll get busy then."

As I go to pass her, she catches my arm. "I know you're one of them, Mercy, at least by blood, but you're one of us too. Whatever you discover down there, remember that life isn't always as simple as life and death and good and bad."

I like simple, but I nod at her, and she lets go of my arm, handing me the torch as she does so. Ares is behind me as we descend into the darkness, his breathing soft and his steps light. We reach the bottom of the stairs and find a library nearly as large as the one above us. We light candles and more torches, but still, the place is eerie. It's been regularly dusted, but there are signs of neglect in the corners, where spiders crawl in their webs.

Shivering, I ignore them all, even though I've never particularly been a fan of spiders, and we go to the shelf Master Snatte indicated. Ares and I place candles all around us to brighten the floor, then sit down and start pulling books off the shelves. Some are in other languages. Ares picks out bits and pieces of these and determines they aren't the books we're looking for. And then we pull down more, all with similar leather binding, most without titles or any indication about who wrote them.

Several books are an accounting of assassinations. The time. The place. The family involved. And sometimes even the assassin responsible for the killing. But none of them feel like what we're looking for. No, what happened to the phoenixes wasn't an assassination. It was something darker.

When I pull out a thin book wrapped in a leather color that's almost golden, my heartbeat picks up. I don't know why I think this is the book, but some instinct I don't understand tells me that it is. Ares is busy reading through another one, and I'm not really sure, so I open it silently and start to read. At first, it doesn't look like much. It discusses different families, even human families, but I recognize many of the family names. The unknown author of the book begins to detail how losing the wrong lords and ladies has led to war and bloodshed. How too many lives have been lost due to some prick gaining control of a manor, the lands, and its people, and ruining the peace so hard-won by all the families.

Then, the author has a list. Twenty families. All names that are easily recognizable, even though some of the family lines had died out. It has notes scribbled beside the lines that had died. Some indicate that their deaths helped the peace in our country, while others hurt it.

It feels strange reading this book. Like I've been a worker with her head down in a factory all my life, and then one day read the notes of my manager and see my world from an entirely different perspective. The writer of the book seems adamant that there was a plan for our country, a future greater than most people could imagine, but it meant protecting the remaining fifteen families at all costs.

Fifteen families. Twelve of which I know still exist. People who secretly run more of our world than anyone could possibly know. There's Rian's family, royalty among the vampires. All of them answer to him. There are three shifter lords, spread out around the United States, with maps indicating where one lord's territory ends and another begins. I know these family lines. I've never seen them as princes to the shifters, but more like the most powerful packs. But the way the book lays it all out, I realize that I've been a bit of a fool. All the shifters do answer to them, in one way or another, so while they might not call themselves princes, they are.

There are more families. Humans. Fae. Demons. Witches and warlocks. All their names are carefully laid out along with family trees that had been updated to include my parents, Bash's family, and even Tasha's family. Whoever had been making this book and keeping it updated seemed to have stopped after that.

I turn to the next page and frown. It's just a list of names. Most of them have been crossed out but are still legible. For some reason, the list creeps me out. It's too long to be a list of assassination targets, unless the person writing the book was some kind of psychopath. And none of the names seem to be linked to the family trees I'd seen before this.

"What the fuck is this?"

Ares looks up. "What did you find?"

"I don't know yet," I tell him, shaking my head as I flip to the next page.

This page doesn't have pictures, names, or lists, so I read it slowly, hoping to figure out what I'm looking at and if it's connected to the phoenixes, or if I'm just wasting my time.

It has been decided by the guild that the twelve families must survive at all costs. Our Seer has made it clear that if one of them should fall, the world as we know it will crumble and that what is rebuilt in its place might not be to our liking. The Seer wasn't clear, but she did say that what would follow the fall of a great family would involve anarchy, death, and the redistribution of power. So, we've had to make some difficult choices.

After discovering the one option to ensure immortality among the powerful families, it has been agreed upon that this knowledge may never leave the families nor the guild. To admit to the decision that was made would change the way we were viewed forever, in an unfavorable light. I admit to having reservations about what we are doing. Although I understand it is for the greater good, my stomach twists at the sight of the chambers that are being built to keep the phoenixes and to drain them regularly. Sometimes I wish I hadn't used my powers to track down the phoenixes. They were already dying out, nearly extinct, and I fear that protecting our way of life will cost us our souls.

My hands tremble. The pages that follow have crude drawings similar to the one I saw in the book about extinct creatures. There is one picture after another of a person strapped in a chair looking ill. Below the image is the name of the person, their family line, and details about them, including age and physical description. Then, in a slightly different color of pen, a date has been etched along with the words, "death by choice."

I'm shivering. I flip through each page, then freeze on one. The woman in the chair...she looks like me. Not a little like me either, but *exactly* like me. She has the same dark hair. The same arch of her brows. Only, she has a look of horror on her face. *Honor Solarius* is written below the picture, followed by her age, date of birth, and her partner, *Tyson Solarius*. A simple word, *"pregnant"* is scrolled beneath the other information, followed by a date etched with "death by choice." Then, *"embryo: missing."*

My heart races. I turn to the next page where a picture of a man has been drawn. He's tall with dark hair, and his eyes look almost black. His hair is wild, and he has a beard that's just as wild. He too is strapped to a chair, and the words *"Tyson Solarius"* have been written beneath his picture, along with the other information that was beneath each other picture. But then, there's something curious. "*Piece of Heart given.*"

Piece of heart given? What the hell does that mean?

"Find anything?" Ares asks.

I look up to realize he's staring at me.

"I think so. I think...I think these might be my parents."

Ares closes the book in his lap and then puts it to the side. He moves slowly, then sits beside me in the ring of candles. He stares down at the picture of my father and his information, then silently flips to the page that has the woman who looks like me. At last, his gaze meets mine. "I think you're right."

My teeth are chattering. "It says she killed herself."

He nods, watching me closely.

"It says my father gave a piece of his heart. Is that possible? Wouldn't that have...killed him? Isn't the only way for us to die to rip out our own hearts?"

"I don't know."

"Damn it." I glare down at the book, feeling lost.

"Can I?" he asks, reaching for the book.

I hand it to him, then stand and begin to pace around the dark library. He says nothing for a long time, but slowly flips through the book. I know this is the smart thing to do. Ares has always been better with books, better at reading and putting things together. But I feel lost. This isn't something I can fight against the way I want to. I want someone to point to a bad guy I can kill to end this whole thing.

Reading? Putting together pieces? It all just makes me feel frustrated and helpless.

Time ticks by. Too much. Ares finally looks up, sighs, and settles back against the shelves.

"What did you figure out?"

He doesn't look like he wants to tell me.

"Ares." His name is almost a threat.

He sighs again. He opens his mouth, closes it, and opens his mouth again.

"Spit it out," I snap, then remember not to be a total bitch. "I'm already stressed out here."

Those soft green eyes of his hold mine with a gentleness that makes my heart ache. "The book is essentially the history of how the remaining phoenixes were rounded up and forced into being blood slaves by the twelve most powerful supernatural families. The berserkers refused. The most powerful fae families did as well, with the exception of a couple. But the rest of the families agreed that their immortality was worth the cost of the phoenixes' freedom. There was a guild member with the rare ability to track. He was forced to use his powers to find the phoenixes, although he wasn't told why they were locating them. Then the phoenixes were rounded up and kept prisoner here, before being loaned out to the families. Your father and mother were among those phoenixes. They were given to the same household. But every phoenix on this list eventually found a way to end his or her own life. The only unaccounted phoenix was you, and the details around your father's death were unusual." He hesitates, then presses on. "They said your mother was no longer pregnant when she died. She could have miscarried, but phoenixes' have the unique ability to transfer their pregnancies to others, and that was suggested as a possibility. Your father, apparently, made a deal with the family that kept him and your mom to let your mom kill herself. He promised there was a way to keep the head of the family alive without needing blood supplements from him. After she was killed, he gave his master part of his heart. The book doesn't say whether it worked or not, but that your father was consumed by ash afterwards, and it was believed he died, and that it was all a trick."

I sit down. Actually, it feels more like my legs crumble beneath me. My head spins with possibilities, with the sadness of the history of my people and what this all means.

"Are you okay?" he asks, his gaze regretful.

I shake my head, then nod. "I have to be."

He crawls across the floor, then pulls me into his lap, holding me tightly. "We're going to figure this out."

I close my eyes and let him hold me for just a moment. A moment where I feel safe. Where the world is black and white and there's no grey in between. I can almost imagine Ares and me as children once more, running through the woods near my house, laughing, so completely unaware of the true darkness our world holds in its shadows.

"So my father... He is my father? That phoenix?"

"It seems likely." Ares strokes my hair.

"And he targeted the guild and will likely target the twelve families on the list now?"

"I think so."

"And is there anything you aren't telling me?"

He stiffens. The words had come out without a thought, but now I look up and meet his eyes.

"What is it?"

He clears his throat. "First of all, your family and Bash's family are all on that list. Your families imprisoned phoenixes."

It's hard to breathe. "And?"

"And the tracker who found the phoenixes...he was Henry."

"Henry?" My voice cracks as I say his name. "*My* Henry?"

He nods.

I push away from him. He calls my name, but I can't stop

as I race up the stairs. I know I'm trying to escape what I've learned and not Ares, but I just keep running. *Henry.* Henry, the captain of my father's guard. The one who taught me about the guild. Who taught me how to fight, how to survive, who made me feel important. *He* helped find the phoenixes? Is that why he told me so little about his time at the guild or what he specialized in?

Outside, I drop to my knees and pull out the daggers he'd given me. "Amatus sum." I speak the words to the magical daggers and feel them vibrate in my hands. *Amatus sum*. Those are the words I have to speak every time I want my daggers to return to me. They're words that Henry enchanted the daggers with.

"I am loved." That's what the Latin words mean in English. Henry thought if I spoke them enough, one day I might believe them.

Tears sting my eyes. *Is any part of my life real?*

6

Ares

I THINK I SCREWED UP. I want to chase Mercy and somehow make the bomb I just dropped on her better, but I'm pretty damn sure I'll mess that up too. So I just grab the book, blow out the candles, and put out the torches. I use the last torch to get up the stairs, then put it out too and head on to the main floor of the guild, trying my hardest to forget the look on Mercy's face. Taking the stairs, I find the right door and knock.

"Come in."

I enter and find Bash and Rian. Rian is sitting at his desk, a mountain of papers in front of him and a look that says he's fighting a headache, and Bash is in one of the chairs across from him, his feet up on the desk, rubbing his eyes.

"That bad?"

Rian nods. "Worse. People are panicking. And we don't

even know if we're warning the right people or not. It's a shitshow."

"I might be able to help with that."

Now Bash is looking at me too.

I hold out the book. "We found out the information we needed. That man is Mercy's dad. His name is Tyson Solarius. Her mother's name was Honor Solarius. Her mother is dead. Her father, apparently, gave his master a piece of his own heart to let his wife die."

"That's...brutal," Rian says.

Bash shakes his head. "Those sick fucks. Who could possibly do that to people?"

"You'd be surprised how little humanity the people we surround ourselves with have," Rian says dryly, and I belatedly think of the prisons beneath his manor. A shiver rolls down my spine. He's right.

"The book also lists the families that were given phoenixes by the guild. I'm guessing those will be the ones targeted." I try to gentle my next words. "Your family and Mercy's family are both on the list."

Bash inhales sharply. "My parents would never..."

"It might have been your grandparents. Most likely it was."

Bash's eyes widen, and then his mouth pulls into a thin line. "My fucking grandpa. The old pervert would absolutely do something like that. And he lived a very long life before unexpectedly getting very sick and dying."

"I'm guessing when his blood source was gone," I say, trying to hide the disgust from my voice.

He nods. "I better warn my family and Mercy's."

Rian stands and indicates for me to follow him to his balcony, so I do, while Bash stays behind and makes his calls.

Outside, it's early morning, so early that it's almost still night, but grey streaks the sky. It feels like a lifetime ago that we were racing here to try to save people we didn't even know if we could save, and yet, nothing has really been resolved. Not really.

"How is she doing?" Rian asks, hands behind his back, staring out at the horizon.

"Okay."

He glances at me. "Ares, one of the best things about you is that soft heart of yours. You see things that the rest of us assholes miss."

I let a slow breath out, deciding to be honest. "She's struggling, feeling lost. I don't think she knows where her alliances stand. Mercy has always been someone who wants life to be simple. To be clear. But as much as her brain tells her that, she only thinks that way because it makes her feel safer. If she had to sit down and say her parents, or the people she thought were her parents, were bad, then she'd crumble. That wall she has built around her heart is weaker than she realizes. As much as she'd never admit it, she needs us. She needs us to be there to remind her that it's okay that this isn't easy, and that she'll get through it."

Rian gives a tired smile. "Then that's exactly what we'll do."

I hesitate, then press on. "We just need to be open to whatever she decides."

He lifts a brow. "Are you saying if she decides to work with those monsters, we should support her?"

"I'm saying that it's too soon to decide who are the monsters in this situation, but the guild isn't exactly coming out smelling good."

"Fair enough," he says softly. "But everything in me says that man wants to drag our Mercy into a battle that has nothing to do with justice and everything to do with revenge."

"Same. Even though reading about what the guild and the families did, I can't say I blame them for wanting revenge."

"Every time I see a truck driver with a massive vehicle who takes up two spots in the front of a parking lot, I want to tear out their throats. Not many people would blame me for finally putting the jackasses in their places, but it doesn't mean it's the right thing to do."

I can't help but smile because this situation is not at all similar to jerks in parking lots, but he knows that, so he's trying to make light of our current problem. "Agreed."

He shakes his head. "But maybe there's another way. Do you think these people can be.. negotiated with?"

They didn't seem like the type to want anything but death, but it's possible. "Maybe."

"Then perhaps we start there. Maybe we can end this thing before more blood is spilled."

"You do realize the families of the people slaughtered here will want revenge too, right?" I say, because no one seems to be thinking about that.

Rian groans and rubs his face, which is unusual for the vampire prince. He must be more worried than he's leading on. "This whole situation is a problem. A problem I wish I could give my full focus."

"What do you mean?"

He avoids my gaze.

"*What do you mean?*" I emphasize each word this time.

Rian finally meets my gaze. "I had to agree to some things to offer Mercy my family's protection."

"What kind of things?" My heart races. *What's he saying?*

"I had to sell my soul."

I'm about to ask him more when Mercy comes exploding into the room, her eyes wild.

"Mercy..." Rian begins.

She cuts him off. "They came for my family."

And she doesn't need to say more before we're all rushing toward her. We're all hoping for the best, but expecting the worst.

7

MERCY

My hands are trembling as I pull up to the gates that surround my parents' house. They've been smashed down, but already the staff is desperately trying to put them back up, although they've been blackened by fire. I stare at the burn marks on the white stone. It feels like a beautiful painting that's been ruined, and yet, I don't feel sad.

I don't know what I feel.

These gates always felt a little like the entrance to my prison. It was a pretty prison, but also a lonely one. The walls and the lands surrounding my parents' castle hold a thousand moments I cried alone. A thousand times I was made to feel not good enough. Like an unwanted freak.

Yet I didn't want this...any of this.

From what I've heard, the blackened gates are only the tip of the iceberg of the destruction The Shadow League inflicted on the place I grew up. Inside things will be worse. How worse? I don't know yet.

"You okay?" Ares asks softly from the back.

My hands tighten on the steering wheel of the SUV, and

I give a nod. "I'll wait to freak out until I know how much damage there was."

Rian takes one of my hands off the steering wheel and holds it in his, squeezing it tightly. "We need to be ready for the worst."

"Always," Bash whispers from the back.

The household staff moves out of the way of our vehicle, giving us enough space to pull through as the guards give me their own worried nods. It feels strange, like I'm living in a nightmare. Just a short time ago, I'd found the book listing the families that had kept phoenixes. I'd seen my family's name on the list and they'd been warned, but some part of me could never imagine that my bio father would hurt these people. The guild, maybe I could understand that, but the people who raised me? It feels like a personal attack when he seemed to be trying to get me on his side. Did he really think this was the way to convince me? Or was he just playing games with my head?

I spent my whole life dreaming that I had another family, one who loved me. Who saw something good inside of me. When I learned about my biological father, there was this soft spot inside of me that thought this thing between us would be easy. That my father was a good guy, and I could be his daughter who was loved and appreciated, maybe even special in some way.

But I should have known better. Nothing in my life has been simple. *Why would this be?*

I keep driving until we reach the front of the palace. The place I grew up in. The place that never felt like home but was. Outside, servants are on their knees scrubbing what can only be blood off the white stone steps. They look up at our SUV as we approach them, and there's fear in their eyes.

Fear. My people are afraid, and the very idea turns my stomach.

"We can just leave," Ares says. "We don't have to go in if you don't want to."

I shake my head. "No, I have to do this." And before I lose my nerve, I turn off the car and throw open my door, climbing out.

My voice shakes a little as I greet the servants. Beth, who is nearly my age and grew up right alongside me, although her mother would never let her play with me. Her mother, Rachel. Bobby, the best stablehand we've ever had. They're all trying to rid this place of all signs of the attack. I almost tell them that even if they erase the blood, it won't erase their memories, but I know better than to say something so useless. Long ago I learned that something might be true, but not everything needed to be said.

"Lady Ravenwood," Rachel says, climbing to her feet with a bow as I go to pass.

I stop and look at her. The wrinkles on her face are deeper and the shadows beneath her eyes darker. "How are they?"

Her gaze drops to my feet. "I shouldn't be the one to..."

My heart squeezes. No one would tell me a thing on the phone. Not even if my family survived. They said it was best that I come. I've never been sent for before. My last call with my parents had made it clear I wasn't a part of this family any longer, so the fact that they wanted me to come...it made me jump in a car and get my ass here as fast as I could.

The guys follow behind me as I walk down the halls. More servants clean streaks of blood off the floors and walls of the hall, and I almost stop and ask them who the blood belongs to. *My family? The servants who cared for me all my life? The guards who let me train with them?* I have no idea. Whoever we lost, it will hurt.

Sara, our head maid, exits a room and freezes when her gaze hits mine. She's wearing an apron covered in blood, and her face is ashen. Her blonde hair has been pulled back, as it always is, but it's messy. Almost like she half-pulled it up and then changed her mind. She's not much older than my mother, but her steps are slow and measured as she approaches me. "Lady Ravenwood," she greets me. She starts to bow, and I catch her before she can hit the ground.

"Sara, that's not necessary," I tell her, my pulse racing.

She leans heavily against me and takes a long moment before she opens her eyes. And when she does, I see that they're filled with tears. "Go to your parent's room."

I hand her to my men, and then I don't know what happens, but I start to run. It's like I can't breathe. Like I can't feel my own feet anymore. I'm just running, racing past people working everywhere, then up the stairs. I stumble on the steps, but I don't slow.

I need to know. I need to see them. I need to know they're okay. They might not love me, but my heart screams the truth: I love them anyway.

The hall outside their room is dark. Two guards stand beside their door, but they take one look at me, then glance away.

I throw open the doors to their room and see the curtains have been drawn closed around their bed. Part of me expects to see the same thing I've seen a thousand times before. My parents together, holding hands, cuddling, smiling. So in love. Caught in a love so deep there's no room for me in it. But I don't care. This is the first time in my life I want to see them, even if they're just falling all over each other.

The fire is burning too low in the fireplace to see anything properly, so I throw open the doors that lead to their balcony, letting light come exploding into the room, and then I go to the drapes of the bed and pull them back too, then turn to my parents.

My mom's spot on the bed is empty. Just...*empty*. The blankets are pulled up neatly as if she'd never been there. My father lies in the other spot. His face is bandaged. His body is bandaged. But blood leaks from beneath the white dressings in a way it shouldn't. In a way that should have been stopped by now, either by magic or science.

"Dad?"

The one unbandaged eye opens, looking groggily at me. My heart races, and I carefully sit down beside him, placing my hand over his. I know he won't want me to touch him. He's never wanted that. Not a hug. Not a hand held. Nothing. But he surprises me by turning his hand around and squeezing mine.

"They killed her," he whispers, his voice filled with pain.

And he doesn't need to tell me who. My vision of him wavers as tears fill my eyes. "Was it peaceful?"

He winces, and his one eye closes. "It was...the opposite of peaceful. I want to die. I want to forget..."

A sob explodes from my chest, and I press my free hand to my mouth. My father hated it when I cried. He'd always tell me there was nothing to cry about. That I looked pathetic. That I needed to learn to be tougher. But he doesn't say that now.

"We made...a mistake."

"I know, dad," I whisper. "I know your parents kept a phoenix prisoner."

He shakes his head, winces, and then lets out a slow breath. "No, we made a mistake...with you. We...blamed you.

Mercy's Rise

We suspected... We knew. But it wasn't your fault. Never your fault."

I stare in shock, not knowing what to say.

His one good eye opens again and locks with my gaze. "We kept him and his wife too, not just my parents. I've lived for so long because of my curse. Would have continued to live for a long time. But your mom was only human when I met her and fell in love, so I wanted her to live as long as I would. We planned to be together forever." He chokes for a moment on the last word. "But I made a deal with the man. I let his wife kill herself. I thought, I don't know what I thought, but he gave your mother a piece of his heart. He said she would live forever then. And then he faded away. We thought he was dead. And that our prayers were answered. But then your mother was pregnant, and we hadn't been intimate, not yet. And we knew."

My head spins. *They were the ones? They did that to my birth parents?*

I wipe more tears from my eyes, not knowing what to say.

"It was our love story." He coughs a little, squeezes my hand tighter. "But it was their nightmare. He wanted me to know what he felt. And now I do. And I know I was wrong, we were wrong, about so many things. About you too, Mercy. You didn't deserve what we did to you. You deserved to...be loved."

I don't know what to say. I don't know what to do. My father is right. He's the villain for my biological father. He and mother took everything from them. Their lives. Their future. Even their child, in a way. And yet, I didn't want the mom who raised me to die. I didn't want my father to be hurting in this bed.

This... It's not the way. *But what is the way?*

"I'm not going to survive this," he tells me.

"You will," I say, wiping tears from my cheeks.

"No." He closes his eye once more. "Not the loss of your mother."

"But...my brother needs you."

"No, he needs you. Promise me, Mercy. Promise you'll be there for him."

"Of course." The promise comes easily. "But you're going to live."

"One way or another, I won't," he says, and his words sound like a promise too.

Something cracks inside of me, and then I'm sobbing. *Really* sobbing. I squeeze my father's hand tighter.

"I love you," he says, his words slurring.

"I love you too," I say, squeezing his hand more tightly.

He squeezes my hand right back, and then his grip goes lax. My gaze moves to him as he falls to the side. I squeeze his hand, but he doesn't respond. "Dad? Dad!"

Everything is a blur after that. I hear myself screaming, over and over again. I shake him. But nothing I do gets him to respond. To breathe.

My men are there, pulling me back. Holding me. A doctor comes and gives me a sympathetic look, and a sheet goes over my father. People come with a bed with wheels to take him out. And I fight my men. I'm kicking. Screaming. Punching. Demanding and pleading. But they keep me away as my father's body is wheeled out.

Then, everyone is gone. It's just us.

I fall to my knees. They sit down around me. My legs are shaking. My entire body is shaking. And I'm saying words, but I don't know what.

"Mercy?"

The small boy's voice makes an unexpected warmth roll

through my body. I slowly look up and see a little boy in the doorway holding a white teddy bear. He looks nothing like me. His eyes are brown like my father's. His hair is pale brown, like my mother's. But the pain and the loss in his eyes...that I recognize.

I open my arms, and to my surprise, he rushes over, and then I'm holding him. He cries, and I cry, and we sit there, surrounded by my men. Two lost souls.

"You're going to be okay," I whisper to him through my tears as I stroke his hair.

And Ares strokes my hair the same way, as if to say I'll be okay too. But I won't. Not for a long time. Not until I handle the phoenixes. Not until I stop the killing. And not until I figure out how to raise a little kid and ensure I don't fuck him up the way my parents fucked me up.

It's all...just too much.

8

MERCY

It's only been three days since my parents' deaths, but it feels like a lifetime. We'd had a small, quick funeral to lay their bodies to rest. There would be a larger funeral for all my parents' family, friends, and subjects to come to, but my aunt would be handling that. She's a busy person, wanting little to do with our family or any responsibility that came with my father's title, but she had agreed to look after Zayn, my brother, until I tied things up with the current situation. It'd felt wrong to leave the boy there. His big brown eyes locked onto me as I'd left, but I knew he'd never be safe, not until I dealt with my father and the other phoenixes. Because who knows who they'll target next. *Will they come back for my brother?*

I have work to do, no matter how my heart aches.

"Do you really think this will help?" Bash asks, his tone gentle, as gentle as it had been since my parents' death.

"I hope so," I tell him. "But I don't know."

We pull into a parking lot in front of a collection of white buildings with neat rows of flowers outside of the little windows with shutters evenly placed in both directions. Fences connect all the buildings, and there's one slightly larger building with the only door to access the whole facility. The place is lovely but has small touches that always remind me a little of a nice prison, even though I try not to think about that.

It's been a while since I'd come here. Since before the God Fire Academy. Since before the guild. And as much as I hate to admit it, I'm pretty sure I was avoiding coming back.

"The spell will work," Ares tells me from the back.

I pull the bottle out of my jacket pocket and stare at it. The potion is blue. Otherwise, there's nothing special about it, and yet somehow it seems sad. Sad in a way I don't completely understand, but sad just the same. Either way, I stuff it back into my pocket and climb out of the car.

The guys follow. Rian is at my side with his hand on the small of my back, Bash is walking slightly ahead and opens the door in front of us, and Ares follows close behind. The receptionist's gaze is immediately on our small group as we approach her desk. I stop in front of her and open my mouth, but I can't seem to form the words.

"We're here to see Henry Wilson. We called ahead," Bash tells her, his voice absolutely confident.

The receptionist takes our IDs and makes us sign in, but her gaze keeps going back to me in a way I find unnerving. When she hands our IDs back, she says, "He'll be glad to see you. He has pictures of you everywhere and often talks about his little Mercy."

If I thought I couldn't feel worse, I was wrong, because I do now. But I give her a small thank you, and she clicks a buzzer that opens the two doors that lead to a white-washed hallway. She calls to a man on the other side of the doors that we're there to see Mr. Wilson. Again, the man gives me a strange look but leads our group down the hall to a room at the end.

I freeze.

The man in white says, "Right in there," gesturing for me to go in, but I seem to be rooted in place.

"It's okay," Bash says, "she just needs a minute."

The man in white gives me a look I can't quite read then turns and walks back to his chair against the wall, picking up a magazine from the seat before sitting back down. I get the sense he's there to both give us privacy and to keep an eye on us, which oddly makes me feel a bit better. At least they seem to be taking care of Henry here.

I hope.

Looking back at the open doorway, I inch forward. I spot a neatly made twin bed with brown blankets and white pillows. But the bed itself is empty. I keep inching forward, spotting a bookshelf against one corner, and then a desk. By the window, a man sits in a rocking chair, staring down at a book in his hand.

I swear my heart stops. Henry. My Henry. He's aged in a way that takes my breath away. His brown hair is no longer streaked with grey. Instead, he's got grey hair, though not much of it is left, deep wrinkles are all over his face, and even his brows have turned grey. I have to swallow around the lump that forms in my throat, but then I spot his clothes. He's wearing dark slacks and a white shirt that seems to have been ironed. My heartbreak changes. Henry always dressed nicely. No matter the occasion, that was just how he was. At least something hadn't changed about him.

"Henry?" I say, my voice coming out soft.

He looks up slowly, placing a bookmark in his book as he does so. "Yes?"

His voice almost breaks me. His deep, soothing voice.

The voice I'd listened to a million times before. A thousand memories hit me at once. A memory of us lying in front of the fireplace, him reading stories from his favorite books. Us training together as he instructed me on what the guild would expect from me. The way he reassured me that I'd be okay, when he'd cover an injury with a band-aid, or when he'd sit with me after something my parents said upset me.

"It's me," I manage.

He tilts his head, studying me. "I'm sorry...I just don't..."

I nod, my chest aching. "It's okay." I move further into the room. "But we're...old friends."

My gaze moves over the room, and I freeze again. On the bookshelf. On the desk. Photos in frames cover most of the space. All photos of me when I was younger. Me laughing. Me the first time he gave me my daggers. Us in front of a little Christmas tree Henry had set up in my room, when I wanted one I could decorate, not just one decorated by my mother and father.

"That's Mercy," Henry says when he notices my gaze on his photos, his voice kind. "My daughter."

I brush a treacherous tear from my cheek. "She looks...happy."

"She's amazing. Strong, brave, incredible."

I blink away more tears. "You must have done a good job with her then."

"No." He rises from the chair. "She was just born good."

I turn to him, and I don't know what to say. We just stare at each other. And I...just don't know. What do I say to the man who shaped me, who changed the course of my life, when he doesn't remember me? Not the me I am now. *If I tell him the truth, will it upset him?*

My mind flashes back to the last time I'd visited. I'd brought him more recent pictures of him and me. More pictures of what I'd been doing. We'd been having a nice time, and suddenly, he'd started screaming and crying. The nurses had needed to give him a sedative to calm him down, then told me it might be better if I left. I don't want to do that this time. I don't want to hurt him in any way.

"Mercy." Ares's voice is soft and gentle. "The potion."

The potion. Right. I could give it to him. But what if it causes him distress? What if it upsets him? That's the last thing he deserves, this good man. Maybe I should just go.

"Mercy?" Henry repeats. His gaze moves over me, and his eyes widen. "*Mercy!*"

I nod, scared. Not knowing what to say or do.

"You've...grown." And a smile breaks over his face.

I nod again, and then he opens his arms, and I don't even know what I'm doing when I rush into them, choking back tears. He holds me the way that only Henry can, squeezing me tightly, whispering about how much I've grown, how much I've changed, and that I've become a beautiful woman.

He must be having a good day. I squeeze him tighter, ignoring the fact that I've cried more this week than I have in my entire life combined. Because with Henry, tears are okay. With Henry, being sad is just an emotion like any other, and I should lean into it, let it happen, and then feel better. At least, that's what he's always told me.

Not that it's enough to heal the screwed-up, emotional mess that I was, that I *am*.

He finally lets me go. "I'm so glad to see you." He frowns, his brows drawing together as he studies me. "But it's been awhile, hasn't it?"

"Yes," I confirm, even though the word brings a wave of regret.

"Because of my mind. Because of the dementia."

"Yes." Then I rush out, "But I would have visited you more, I just ran into...some trouble."

He nods, then sits back in his chair. "Tell me what's going on."

I sit on the edge of his bed, as close to him as I can get, wishing I could hug him again. Wishing I could stay in this moment forever. "Mom and dad have died."

Wincing, I immediately wish I could take the words back. My purpose here isn't to hurt him. It isn't to stress him out.

But instead of falling apart like last time, he gives a grave nod. "What happened?"

I hesitate and look at Ares. He nods, and so I force myself to turn back to Henry. "I discovered that my father, the beast himself, wasn't my real father. I'm actually a phoenix. And my biological father isn't dead. He's alive. And angry. He's created a group to try to get revenge on all the families that imprisoned phoenixes for their blood. According to some of the victims, they've made it clear this is only the beginning, and they won't stop until every last person associated with the twelve families is dead."

Henry's eyes are wide. "I'm so sorry, Mercy. This is all my fault. I never wanted it to lead to this. But it's my fault."

"Because you tracked the phoenixes?"

He hesitates, looking surprised, then says, "Yes. The guild asked me to. I didn't know why at first, but my gut told me not to. Still, I did it, and so everything that followed afterward is my fault."

Of course, they didn't tell him. Henry would never have participated in something like this if he realized what the families had planned for the phoenixes. Of that I have no doubt. And with no links to a powerful family himself, he wouldn't have been able to do anything to stop what happened after.

"You're not to be blamed for what they did to the phoenixes," I tell him, a little anger rushing into my voice. There is no way in hell I'm going to let one old man blame himself for everything that happened. There's plenty of blame to go around, but none belongs to him.

He shakes his head. "You don't understand. My kind...trackers...our abilities are rare and highly sought after. My father told me to take what I am to my death, but it was the only way to get into the guild, so I told them. I sold my secret for a chance at freedom, a chance to work for a family like yours. I knew better, but I did it anyway."

I reach out and take his hand, squeezing it. "You're a good person, Henry. That's one of the few things I know for sure in this world."

He smiles at me, and his blue eyes sparkle. "I've missed you."

"I've missed you too. I'm so sorry I haven't come to visit. I'll do better in the future."

"Mercy." He says my name with such affection that I wish I could bottle the word and play it over and over again any time I feel lost and alone. "This is the future for all trackers. Our unique abilities are hard on our minds. I always knew this is where I would end up. I hoped I had more time, but life had other plans. The thing is that I have some good moments, but they don't last long, so it's important that I tell you everything I need to tell you before it's too late."

"Of course," I say, but something in my gut clenches. I don't know why. Maybe because the man I love and admire had used an ability that he knew would destroy his mind, and did it anyway, and I'm not sure how I feel about that. Maybe...sad because I would have had more time with him if he hadn't. Or maybe relieved that I didn't have to give him a potion to get him to remember, but worried because now he's going to tell me things, possibly things I don't want to know.

Usually, this would be the time I ran for it. But I'm not running from this. I *can't* run from this. Not when so much hangs in the balance of what this man might be able to tell me.

"Mercy, there are a lot of things I know in this world. Things that you can only truly understand through life experiences. I know that you feel safer in a world where things are black and white. You've always been that way, but it's time for you to grow up." He doesn't say it unkindly, if anything his voice is regretful. "Lord and Lady Ravenwood were not bad people, but they also weren't good people. They were kind to their subjects, and horrible to you. They loved each other in such a deep way that people wrote stories about them. But they witnessed the love between Honor and Tyson Solarius, your biological parents, and they couldn't've cared less. I wasn't there when Tyson made the deal with your father to kill his wife. I never saw Honor and Tyson again after I tracked them to their home and let the guild know where they were. Everything after that was done quietly. But even when I watched them, I knew that they loved each other. For your father and mother to see that and not care, to be willing to let one of them kill herself so violently just to escape the hell they put her through..." Henry's face flashes with rage.

"That's awful," is all I can manage.

He nods and shakes himself, as if remembering where he is. "But I researched Tyson after I tracked him down. He was...also not a good person."

Both my dads were jerks? Seriously? "How so?"

Henry's soft brown eyes meet mine. "He wasn't a stranger to murder, theft, or torture. Your mother seemed to be an innocent in all of his actions, but he was not a good man. What happened to him, no one deserves that, but if you're trying to decide which side to fall on in this fight, don't choose his. I'm not saying to not help the phoenixes, but don't choose his side."

I frown. "But he and the phoenixes are one."

"Are you sure?" He's studying me in that way he always used to do, like he's waiting for something to click with me. Something I don't understand.

"It seems that I'm either going to have to help stop them, or help them win. I don't see another option."

He reaches out and takes my hand, squeezing it tightly. "Look in the grey, Mercy. You've spent all your life avoiding it, but you have to look in the grey now."

"But no solution is a good one," I tell him, feeling my heart race.

"Maybe not, but there has to be a solution you can live with. I know you've done a lot of things in your life that you aren't proud of, but you're nothing like the lord and lady, or your biological parents. You're you. Make the decision that's right for you."

I feel tears sting my eyes. "I want to understand, but I don't. I want to be like you and live in the grey, but I can't." My chest feels strangely tight. "The phoenixes are going to keep killing until they're stopped. They'll probably even come back for my brother. And then the families will want their revenge. They'll use spells to track them and send hellhounds after the phoenixes until they're all rounded up. Unless I step in. I just don't know...how to step in. I don't know what's right."

His hand squeezes mine more tightly. "I've always seen

you as my daughter. You've always made me proud. I know you'll make me proud now too. You'll figure out what's right."

I think he's wrong, but I don't want to waste anymore of his good time on this. "I love you."

"I love you too."

We spend some more time together. I ask him about his time at the care home, and he tells me stories. He admits that a lot of it is a blur, but that overall, he's happy. He's made a few friends, and life is quiet and peaceful. Then, he turns to my guys, who I'd almost forgotten.

"And who are they? Are you dating one of them?"

"All of us, actually," Rian says in a matter-of-fact way.

"Really?" Henry's brows lift, and then he laughs. "I always said no man would be good enough for my Mercy, so maybe three will be."

Rian smiles right back. "Pretty sure she could add on another one of us."

And then, everyone is laughing.

Henry turns back to me. "So, what have you been doing?"

"I got into the guild after the academy," I tell him, pride in my voice. Not that I'd been some major success story there, but he doesn't need to know everything.

"The guild?" He frowns.

"Yeah." I stare at him for a minute, but he still looks confused.

"Oh, yeah, right, the guild." He smiles again, then turns toward the door. "And, who are your friends?"

Uh. "You remember Bash and Ares, and then that's Rian." Yeah, I could have introduced him as a vampire prince, but I'm getting the sense that Henry might be feeling a bit overwhelmed.

"Bash and Ares?" He sounds unsure.

"Yeah, we all grew up together."

"Oh, right, right." But he doesn't seem like he remembers.

"I love you, Henry." I don't know why it slips out again, but my palms are suddenly sweaty.

"I love you too," he tells me, but this time his smile feels a little forced. "And you know, you remind me so much of someone. A little girl I used to spend time with. Her name is Mercy."

My stomach flips.

Ares comes forward and sits down beside me on the bed, putting a hand lightly on my knee. "She's heard that before."

"She was a lovely little girl. Stubborn, wild, but lovely."

I can't seem to find the words to answer him. This is what Henry was like the last time I visited. But for some reason, I felt like this visit was different. Like the Henry I knew was back. And watching him slip away now feels like I'm losing him all over again.

"You must have had some fun times," Ares says, his rare smile gentle as he looks at Henry.

"We did," Henry rises, but he seems unsteady on his feet. Bash is there in an instant, helping him walk over to the pictures on his dresser. Henry starts to tell stories from the pictures, but none of them sound quite right. He's mixing things up. Important things I never thought he would forget.

But I'd made peace that he'd forgotten so much of our lives together. *So, why am I upset now?*

Henry suddenly says, "I'm tired. Can you guys leave so I can lay down?" And he's not smiling any longer. If anything, he looks angry.

Ares and I get off the bed, and Bash helps him over to it. Henry sits down carefully at the edge, and his eyes close for a long moment before he looks up at us. There's no recognition in his eyes. "Is it pudding day? I really want pudding, but not vanilla. You always give me vanilla, and I want chocolate."

"Chocolate it is," Rian says, then disappears out into the hall.

Henry looks at us again. "And my sheets need another washing, and I want breakfast, and it's too bright in here."

I'm just staring, frozen, but Bash launches into action. He closes the blinds and draws the curtains, making it darker, then helps to pull back the sheets and blankets on his bed on the other side of Henry. He kneels down and helps Henry remove his shoes while Henry frowns down at him, and Ares wraps an arm around my back while I stare, unsure of what to do. Bash helps to adjust Henry beneath the covers, pulling them up to his chest.

A minute later, Rian is back. He has about two dozen chocolate pudding cups in his arms, and he looks pissed. He takes them to the dresser and lets them spill over it. "Chocolate pudding cups, as requested."

Henry's eyes light up. "Chocolate pudding is my favorite, but they never let me have it. They give it to the others first."

Rian lifts a brow. "I've spoken to them. You will be given as much chocolate pudding as is healthy for you. I have their word on that." Then, he takes a spoon wrapped in plastic out of his back pocket and brings Henry a cup of pudding and the spoon.

Henry wraps his hands around them, lays back, and closes his eyes. "I'm going to have this. After a little rest. Just a little one."

Bash pats him on the shoulder. "You rest. The pudding will be here when you wake up."

And then Henry's head falls to the side, and I watch the steady rise and fall of his chest.

I realize I'm shaking, and I have no idea why. Moving to his side, I stare down at him. I want to touch him, but don't, because I don't want to startle him awake. Instead, I slip the potion out of my pocket and hide it in the back of his nightstand. Someday, when he needs a good day, I'll remind him it's there.

Looking down at him, I swear my heart bleeds.

Ares puts his arm around me and leads me out of the room, followed by Rian and Bash. When we pass the nurses' station, there are two nervous-looking nurses and a pile of pudding cups scattered on the counter. They take one look at Rian and tense. I want to ask him about it, but I don't feel like I can. We head to the front desk where the same woman who checked us in is waiting.

Bash moves to stand in front of her, flashes a smile that has an edge of a warning, and says, "That man, Henry, is beloved by very powerful people. I hope none of your staff are foolish enough to forget that."

Her eyes widen and she gives a sharp nod, and then we're outside.

I don't know why, but I pull away from Ares. I start toward the car, then pace away from it. My clothes feel too tight, and I can't seem to catch my breath. I just keep pacing, trying to remember to take deep breaths.

"It's a lot," Bash says softly, and my gaze jerks to him. "Henry was a strong man, a powerful man. He taught all of us so many things about fighting. He taught Ares and me about what it meant to be men. But the best thing he ever did was raise you. Without him, I don't know what would have happened."

"I know that," slips from my lips, and my eyes blur with tears.

"It's nice that after all the hard things he seems to have gone through, most of the memories he's left with are about you. Even now, you're the best thing in his life. And he has a nice, safe place to enjoy those memories."

I nod, taking a shaky breath in.

"Should we go?" Ares asks gently.

Rian answers for us. "Probably. I just put the fear of God into a bunch of nurses when I learned that they were prioritizing the chocolate pudding for other patients. They're likely watching us right now, hoping I don't come back."

And for some reason, I give a sob that's half a laugh. "You guys are ridiculous."

They smile back at me, and this time, I feel like I can go to the car. Because even though seeing Henry like that is hard, they're right. He's safe. And he has some good memories to keep him company.

Plus, if I can solve the problem of the phoenixes and the powerful families, I should be able to come see Henry more. And every time I feel like I can't handle anything more, I can remember the way Ares touched me, grounding me, with Henry. The way Bash took care of the older man I love so much. And the way Rian scared the hell out of a bunch of nurses to ensure the man I love got his pudding.

A girl could do worse.

9

MERCY

We're all on edge as we pull outside the gates to Rian's castle. I'm not one hundred percent sure what's going on in my guys' heads, but I'm a complete mess. My father, no, Tyson Solarius, the phoenix, has never been a good person. He'd had horrible things happen to him, so while that might explain why he is the way he is, it still didn't justify it. And the father who raised me, the beast himself, had tried to make amends with me before he died.

For some reason, when I think of him and my mother, I no longer feel angry. I just feel...sad. The way they treated me all my life could, again, be explained by my mom becoming pregnant with me against her will, and not being either of their biological child, but it didn't justify the cruelty they showed me.

"Do you--?" I realize I'm about to speak aloud and stop myself, but everyone has already heard me.

"Do you what?" Bash asks, a small smile stretching his lips.

Well, hell, I can't back down now, can I? "Do you think that maybe I don't need to see Tyson or Lord Ravenwood as my father...but Henry instead?"

To my surprise, it's Bash who speaks. "If life has taught me anything, it's that family isn't about who you share blood with. It's about who you love." He gives me a pointed look before continuing. "I love my family, but I was mostly raised by maids and nannies. And the second they could, they shipped me off to train with Rian, Ares, and you. So when I think about my family, I don't exactly have negative thoughts toward my parents, but I definitely think about the three of you instead."

"Awww, how sweet!" Rian exclaims.

Bash punches him in the arm from the back seat, and we're all laughing.

And then, Ares says, "Wolves always say nothing is more important than your pack. Well, my pack threw my father and me away, so I've chosen all of you as my pack now. So why can't Henry be your father too? I'd welcome him into our pack."

"Besides, it's clear he sees you as his daughter, so why not?" Bash adds.

I smile. "Next time I see him, I'm going to tell him as much."

The gates finally part in front of us and we see several guards ahead waiting on the other side. Rian rolls down his window, and they quickly gesture for him to go ahead. Still, it's weird. There's definitely a change in the air that I don't completely understand, and I'm damned sure there are multiple lookouts in the trees that we drive past. Apparently, the other houses aren't the only ones tightening their security.

We're nearly to the front of the mansion when Rian curses.

"What?" I ask, every muscle in my body tightening.

Rian points to a white sports car pulled up outside the castle. "Apparently, my father is back..."

I look at the other guys. "How bad is that?"

Bash's face gives nothing away. "We'll see."

We climb out of our car and head inside. And maybe it's my imagination, but the servants are rushing around in a way I never imagined. There's an underlying...almost terror, that makes me wonder if Rian's father has earned his reputation of being fearsome honestly, and also how the hell Rian ended up so much gentler.

"Mercy, just think before you talk," Rian says softly, almost under his breath.

I lift a brow. "Don't I always?"

"No," they all say together.

"Three freaking stogies," I mutter.

Bash flashes me a grin. "Or we all just agree on the same thing that's very obvious to everyone outside of you." Then his grin fades away. "And King Drakkar is not the person for you to piss off. Trust us."

"No, he is not." A man comes from around a corner, and every muscle in my body stiffens. He looks...so much like Rian. Most vampires tend to be thinner, paler, and very clean-cut. Rian's father has a similar build to Rian himself, which is far bulkier than most vampires, definitely closer to the body of a shifter. Both of them have brown eyes ringed by red, and the same shade of dark brown hair. Even the sharpness of their faces is eerily similar, except that while Rian has a beard that gives him a wilder edge, his father's face is cleanly shaven.

His dark eyes swing to his son. "Welcome home."

Rian gives a little nod that's almost a bow, his back is oddly stiff.

"This is uncomfortable."

All eyes turn to me.

I shrug. "What? It is. And with the awkward relationship I had with my parents, if I notice something is up, something is really up."

The vampire king's gaze focuses on me. "You must be Lady Ravenwood."

"Call me Mercy," I say.

"No," he tells me simply, then continues on as if I hadn't spoken. "I heard about the loss of your parents. It's a terrible tragedy."

I almost snort but manage to hold back, even though I'm one hundred percent sure that King Drakkar couldn't give a shit about my parents. "Thanks."

"You're also an important woman to my son, it seems." His gaze trains on my face, and I keep my expression carefully blank. If this guy thinks I'm some wilting flower he'll be able to stare at until I crack, he has no idea what I'm made of.

"Does it?" I ask him, lifting a brow.

We have an intense moment when we're both staring at each other before Bash suddenly says, "It's good to see you back home, King Drakkar," then bows.

"I hope your journey was pleasant, Your Highness," Ares adds on, giving his own little bow.

I almost sigh. Part of me had forgotten this world after so long at the academy and then at the guild. There's just so much pomp. So much formality. Which is basically ass kissing.

"It was pleasant," the king says with a smile that seems cruel. "But then, finally telling all our subjects that my son will be taking over the throne and ruling our people is quite a cause for celebration."

"You did what?" I ask, turning to Rian and feeling angry for some reason. I understand that he doesn't need to tell me everything, but for some reason, I feel like we're at a point in our relationship where I'd at least hear about a major decision like this, and I'm about to tell him exactly that.

Instead, Ares says, "We should probably clean up after our journey."

"Of course," the king says, "and then join me for dinner. We have a lot of important things to discuss."

I want to tell him to shove it, that *we* have some important things to discuss, but even though I'm an idiot sometimes, I'm not *that* stupid, so I just shut my mouth. Servants lead me to a room, because, apparently, the guys already have rooms here, and then another servant comes with various clothes in my size, mostly things I'd actually wear. Which is surprising, but nice.

So, I take a quick shower and then change into a purple blouse and slacks. Yeah, it isn't leather, but dining with a king has certain requirements. No matter how much I hated it, I always tried to dress nicely for my parents' important guests.

A pang rings through my heart when I think of my parents, and suddenly, I realize I'm sitting on the edge of the bed. I have no idea how long I've been there, but I'm just staring down at my hands. Someone knocks lightly at my door, and I call for them to come in, confused about what I'm doing.

Ares is standing in the doorway wearing black pants and a button-up green shirt that makes his eyes pop. He looks clean, handsome, and yet, still, somehow, nervous. *How can he possibly be so beautiful it hurts to look at him sometimes, and still not seem to realize it?*

"You alright?" he asks, his voice oddly soft.

"You're ridiculously handsome and need to stop being so insecure. It's driving me crazy."

His eyes widen. "Uh, thanks? I mean, I'm sorry."

I shake my head. "Sorry, I didn't mean to say that out loud."

He closes the door behind him and moves closer until he's standing right in front of me. "What are you up to?"

"I don't know. I was getting ready for dinner, even put on these stupid clothes, and I was thinking about dinners with my parents and their important guests. Then, I was just sitting here. I have no idea why."

He kneels down in front of me, and I realize I only put one of my boots on. He takes the sock still lying on the ground and puts it on my bare foot, then pulls my boot on and starts to lace it up.

"I'm not a child," I say, even though it feels oddly nice to have him take care of me like this.

"I know," he says, then ties my boot.

"And I'm not sad about my parents."

Those bright green eyes of his meet mine. "I know."

Tears blur my vision. "I'm not weak."

"I know." He stands and then sits next to me on the bed, wrapping an arm around my back.

I lean into him. "We need to go to dinner."

"Yes, we do. But not yet. Not until you're ready."

So, we sit together for a while. No tears fall. The ones in my eyes clear, but I still can't seem to move. The thing is, I'd have thought a moment like this would be uncomfortable. It's not. Having Ares here with me just feels natural. And that alone is enough to make me feel more like myself. To remember that my life might be unstable right now, but Ares is the most stable person I've ever met.

I stand, straightening my back. "I'm okay."

He stands too and offers me his arm. "I'll be there with you the whole time."

I give him a look, knowing there's more he wants to say. "What do you want to remind me about?"

"Just that you should call Rian Prince Drakkar, and that you should remember that the vampire king is not a patient or kind man. He isn't cruel, per se, but he is not someone that you want to get snarky with."

"Snarky? Me?"

He laughs, and some of the tension I'd felt in my chest eases.

I can't help it, so I ask, "Did you know Rian had agreed to be king?"

"Just recently," he says with a shrug.

"Why didn't he tell me?"

He avoids my gaze. "It's complicated."

"You know I'm not leaving it at that..."

He gives me a smile that makes me feel warm. "I know, but we're going to be late. Can you launch my interrogation later?"

"Fine," I tell him, then take his arm.

We leave my room, and I rub the spot above my heart, wondering why the hell I always feel pain there when I think of my parents. *Maybe I need to see a doctor?*

We go down the stairs and then enter the dining hall, where everyone is standing around the table having wine, or blood, depending on if they're a bloodsucker or not. It's the king himself, our mighty prince, Bash, and Ares's father. Ares and I pause when we enter the room, and then all eyes turn to us. I avoid most of the gazes, but I can't help looking at Ares's father.

I'd met him a few times before when he briefly visited

Ares when Ares would come to our home to train, and his father hasn't changed much. The man is...formidable. Large in all ways. And he looks nothing like Ares. But I've seen pictures of Ares's mother and know exactly who he took after.

His father tilts his head slightly as he regards me. It shifts the long red hair that falls around his shoulders and weaves in with the long red beard on his chin. His green eyes, which are admittedly the same shade as Ares's eyes, regard me with interest and perhaps a little disappointment. But that's one thing I always seem to connect with his father, disappointment when he looks at me. He wears a dark grey shirt and slacks, but he looks like he's been squeezed into them. Like his huge muscles weren't meant to be bound by clothes. But then I guess it makes sense. When the king is as big and strong as he is, he needs someone bigger and stronger to be his protector, and there's probably a short list of people who meet that expectation.

Ares nudges me a little and then starts to guide me toward the group of dinner guests. A servant meets us halfway, offering us both white wine, which I gladly accept, but then choose not to chug it, even though I'm feeling nervous. When we reach the others, everyone exchanges formal greetings, and I get another "*Sorry* about your parents" from Ares's father, which I try to accept without noticing the ache in my chest.

And then, we sit down around a grand dark wood table covered in candles, a blazing fire to our side. A woman with a harp comes and settles into one corner and begins to softly play a sad song. The first course brought out is an amuse-bouche, which sits in a little porcelain spoon. We, of course, wait for the king to try his food first, then once he's done, we each try our own. To no one's surprise, it's awesome.

More courses come out while everyone makes small talk. It doesn't feel exactly like the king is avoiding the more serious topics, more like he has a specific time in place to discuss it, which my father also loved to do, so I try to keep my mouth shut and just watch everyone.

I hear Ares say to his dad, "How's the garden doing?"

His dad smiles. "Well, Martha takes care of it when I'm gone, but it always needs a little extra love and care when I get back."

"And Speed?"

Speed is the name of the horse Ares usually likes to ride when he's home, although I know he's getting too old to be ridden. I overheard Ares telling Bash that he usually just takes him for walks and feeds him apples and his other favorite treats every time he visits.

"He's slowing down, but still smart as ever," his dad says. But when his gaze meets mine, the smile drops from his face, and he quickly looks away from me.

Right, the guy thinks I'm trouble and wants me to stay the hell away from his son. Message received. He doesn't need to keep politely treating me like a turd everyone's *gracefully* kicking away from them underneath the table. I get it.

So, I focus on Rian, Bash, and the king. They're discussing the different properties and businesses that are owned by the Drakkar family. Apparently, the king still plans to keep an eye on them but has his sights set on retiring on a small island the family owns that he's been building a massive mansion on for years. It's finally ready, and he plans to go there after the coronation in less than a week. He assures Rian that he'll continue to check in and help, but that he's nearly one hundred and fifty and feels ready to enjoy his life a little.

Rian, for his part, mostly just nods, but I can sense a strange sadness beneath his surface. He agreed to be the new king of the vamps, without even discussing it with the rest of us, so why does he seem to be sad about it? It makes no sense to me, but I manage to keep my thoughts to myself.

For now.

Finally, dessert is served. Some chocolate dish with flecks of real gold, and, apparently, a syrup of blood, for Rian and his father. I taste mine, really hoping my syrup is some kind of berry, and then release a slow breath when strawberries and chocolate hit my tongue. Bash's gaze locks with mine, and he grins, I'm pretty sure because he's read my damn mind.

As we eat, the feeling in the room changes. The king glances at us, then his son. "So, did Rian speak to you about our agreement?"

Agreement? "Not yet," I say, and Bash and Ares say the same, while Ares's father suddenly seems fascinated by his dessert.

"My son has agreed to waive all his prior requests about how he wants our system changed and accept his role as king." There's a slight smugness to his voice that I don't like.

I think back to my conversation with Rian. He'd seemed dead-set on changing the vampire's system. On making it illegal to own blood slaves, to feed on unwilling humans, etc. *What could possibly have happened to make him change his mind?*

King Drakkar's gaze moves to me. "Which is why I was so fascinated with you."

"With me?" I ask, lifting a brow.

He picks up his crystal goblet full of blood and smiles

before taking a sip. "Yes. I have tried everything I could imagine, save killing Rian and siring another heir, to get him to be reasonable, but nothing worked. And then he asks that I add spells to protect you from hellhounds and allow you sanctuary here, and he'll do anything I ask. It was...a surprise. A pleasant one."

I feel the color drain from my face and whirl to face Rian. "Is that true?" There's a harshness to my voice I know I shouldn't be using on a prince, but I don't give a damn right now.

"It's...complicated. We'll discuss it later."

"*Later*?" I almost shriek the word.

Someone kicks me under the table, but I don't care. "I think we should discuss this right *now*. No, actually, I think we should have discussed this before you made a life-changing decision."

"So you are romantically involved?" The king sounds amused.

"We won't be tonight," I shoot back.

The whole table is awkwardly silent for so long that even I realize it, and then King Drakkar throws back his head and laughs. "I was a little worried about my son choosing a phoenix, but my worries have eased. Your kind are rare, powerful, and you will live as long as my son. And with that attitude, I fully believe you'll be able to handle the role of a woman on my son's arm."

"Mercy," Rian says my name in a low, dangerous way that has my body humming. "You really want to discuss this now?"

I cross my arms over my chest. "As a matter of fact, I do."

Rian gives a jerky nod, then turns to face his father. "Actually, I don't intend to have Mercy be like the many women who have been on your arm over the years. I plan to marry her."

"*Marry?*" The word comes out really high pitched. It's a pitch that would make a dog bark, but I can't help it.

"Marry," his father repeats, but he's staring hard at his son. Whatever he sees in Rian's face, he suddenly leans back in his chair, almost collapsing. "You're serious?"

"I am," Rian says, a challenge in his voice.

"Doesn't the lady in question get a vote in this?" I sputter out.

They both ignore me, and the father says, "Well, if Mercy is to be your bride, I guess she should know about all the dark little secrets of this place. She should know that this isn't some fairy tale castle like the one she grew up in. Or do you think she can't handle that?"

"First of all," I began, my heart racing, "I didn't grow up in some fucking fairy tale. Second of all, I can handle every dark, creepy thing this place has hiding in its shadows. And, third of all, I haven't even agreed to marry him!"

I feel really proud of my argument, but neither of them are looking at me. Instead, Ares and Bash are giving me looks of pity, like I'm on some roller-coaster I can't get off of and I'm the only stupid kid who seems to think there's an eject button, which I don't appreciate one bit.

"She can handle it," Rian tells his father, then sips his own goblet of blood.

The king stands. "Then, let's take a little tour. Shall we?"

Rian's eyes darken and the red rings around his pupils spread, "Is this necessary?"

"If you say the word, it isn't."

They glare at each other, and then Rian stands and offers me his hand. "Come."

"I'd rather stay," I tell him with a smirk. "Or whatever other commands you give dogs."

I actually think I hear Rian's teeth clench together.

Everyone else gets up, and Ares gives me a warning look. Not his usual one, but a look that makes my palms feel clammy. Is this one of those situations I don't completely understand but that's going to end badly if I don't play along? Probably. So, reluctantly, I stand.

Rian takes my hand and wraps it around his arm, and then his father leads us out of the dining hall, with Ares's father at the back of our little group. We're led through the mansion to a back set of stairs that, apparently, go to some kind of basement. But I'm not paying as much attention to my surroundings as I usually do, which wouldn't make Henry happy at all. Instead, my brain is in overdrive. *Marry? Rian? Be some kind of vampire queen? See all their dark secrets? What the hell is happening?*

We get to the bottom of the stairs and are met with a big metal door. There doesn't seem to be a lock of any kind. Instead, the king simply spins the metal wheel on it, and the door comes popping slowly open like a bank vault. I'm oddly focused on what the hell they're locking down here like this when I hear moaning and wailing. It isn't loud. Not like someone is being actively tortured. It's almost like the sounds you encounter when coming to a pound late at night. Like all the animals have just given up, but they're still miserable.

I don't like it one bit.

But when we actually walk into the basement, my hand drops from Rian's arm and I just stare and stare. It's one long hallway, with a couple of other hallways branching off of it, lined with prison cells. I'm the only one who moves forward as I walk down the hall like I'm in a nightmare, glancing into each cell to see a sickly-looking person, probably a human, with bruises covering their throats and wrists. All of them are alive, but so pale that I actually have to watch for the rise and fall of their chests to be sure that they're still alive.

I spin around. No one will look at me except the king. "What the fuck is this?"

Rian's gaze darts up and he opens his mouth, but his father answers. "Our blood slaves. Like most great families, we have them. But Rian has always had an issue with our ways. When he was younger, he actually let them all go. We managed to round up most of them once more, but it was then that I knew my son's heart was far too soft to help him become a great leader. So, I killed the remaining blood slaves to teach him a lesson that whatever he thought he was doing, he just made things worse for them." He pauses and looks at Rian. "But in exchange for your safety, he has agreed to never let these slaves go again. To respect that they are our property. And, with that agreement in line, and several others, I will not only offer you sanctuary here, but knowledge. I have discovered a powerful secret. A spell that would allow you to become untraceable to the hellhounds and to anyone else. You'd be free to go wherever you want, whenever you want. Both Rian and I have come to the understanding that this piece of information is the only one that will allow you any freedom, and I will give him the spell after his coronation."

I'm shaking, barely understanding what he's saying. Images of phoenixes in cages like these roll through my mind, and I know one thing: I will free these people. Not stupidly. Not right now when they'll just be caught again, but I will. And even though my heart is screaming to tear into the king, I force a smile. "So this was your big secret?"

King Drakkar's surprise isn't hard to see. "Yes. One of ours."

I shrug. "Well, thank you for showing me, but it has been a long day."

Bash surprises me by speaking. "Also, these blood slaves were just fed on, so they're in the worst shape. If you keep going through the basement, you'll see that they've made homes in their cells and that most are treated fairly well." His expression says that he doesn't agree with it, but wants to make sure I fully understand the situation.

"Of course," I tell him, even though that doesn't make any of this okay.

The king leads us back upstairs, while I give a final glance at the people in the cells. *Okay, I handled this well. I didn't raise suspicion. But I'll be back here soon, and when I come back, no one will be left here in pain, no matter how I have to free them.*

Upstairs, we all go our separate ways, except Rian, who takes my hand and puts it in his arm once more before leading me upstairs. Once we reach my room, he closes the door softly behind us, and I whirl around to face him, fuming. "What the hell?"

He actually looks upset. "I know I should have told you, but then you would have refused my help."

"Damn-freaking-right!"

"And we needed this place for you. We needed you to be safe."

"I can fucking take care of myself!"

He gives me a look, then keeps going. "What's more, this was inevitable. Me becoming king. I had hoped to get some of the things I wanted before agreeing to become king, but I'm also determined to find ways around my promises."

"Loopholes?"

He nods and some of my anger fades.

"I can help you find loopholes."

He moves closer to me. "I know you can."

"And what's with all the wedding stuff?" I ask, feeling nervous as he closes the space between us.

"It was something the boys and I discussed. One of the few ways of keeping you safe. Now, it's not just that you're a phoenix and people can track your magic. Too many people actually know that Mercy Ravenwood is a phoenix. But as my wife, even the temptation of a phoenix wouldn't be enough for most people to have the entire vampire race hunting them. So, it's a way to keep you safe."

"I never planned to be a wife."

He smiles. "I never planned to have a wife, but somehow, I think we'd make a good match."

"I don't know..." I'm shaking my head, actually feeling tired now.

He reaches for me and pulls me into his arms. "Nothing needs to be decided tonight. Tonight, we can just rest."

I close my eyes. "But there's so much to do."

"There's always so much to do."

Then, I remember something else. "What about this spell? The one that's supposed to make it so no one can track me?"

He hesitates, and I open my eyes, staring up into his face. "My father had to use a lot of his connections to find it and pay an incredible price, but I'm certain it's real and that he'll follow through with his word and give it to me after my coronation. It's his way of ensuring I don't back out of it, because it's one of the only ways to make sure you're truly safe."

"You didn't have to do that for me."

He strokes my face. "Yes, I did."

Damn him, he's so sweet. It makes it hard to be mad at him. "Is there anything else you haven't told me? Have you decided our kids' names? Did you buy a house somewhere?"

He laughs. "No." Then, his laughter fades away. "Well..."

"Rian..." There's a light knocking at my door. "Come in," I call, instantly ready for some new danger.

Instead, Bash comes in looking as tired as I feel. "I just wanted to check on you."

Rian sits down in a chair near the fire and pours himself a glass of brandy, then begins to sip it while staring at the fire. I get the strong impression he's trying to melt into the background and give us time to talk, while also staying close to me. Which makes me a little worried.

I turn to face Bash. "I'm okay. The marriage stuff, and everything else, was just a bit of a surprise."

He nods, then draws his shoulders back. "I know you kind of see me as an asshole–"

"*Kind of?*" I ask, lifting a brow.

But he doesn't smile. "I just want you to know that none of us are okay with the blood slaves. If we thought we could free them and have them be safe, we would. But Rian tried it before, and the king killed all of the ones that were tracked down. That was a lesson all of us have never forgotten."

I realize he's serious and cross the room toward him, letting my hands move down his big arms. "Bash, you're an asshole, but you have an incredible heart. I know you wouldn't willingly let something like that happen if you had any other choice."

Bash still holds himself tensely. "Life isn't always easy or simple."

What's going on with him? Is he really worried that I think badly of him? "You sound like Rian."

He completely disregards my teasing words. "What's

more... The marriage stuff. I don't want you to think that means Ares and I are just walking away. If you agree to it, you'll be Rian's wife in name, but we want you to be...ours too."

"Sweet talker," I tease him, feeling uncomfortable with all the talk from Bash.

Those pale green eyes of his hold mine, no hint of humor, just sincerity. "You have no idea how much you mean to me. How much it hurt to be away from you for so long. How hard it was when you hated us." His voice breaks a little.

Damn it. He's not going to let this go. I guess my big man's soft heart came out, so I'll have to let mine out a little too.

I lean up onto my tiptoes and wrap my arms around him, holding him closely. "I know. It wasn't easy for me either."

"It felt like we ripped out our own hearts," he whispers, then pulls me into his arms. "You're annoying, stubborn, and not the least bit funny–"

"Hey!" I mutter against his shoulder.

"But you're ours. And we're yours. Always and forever."

I shift so that I can see him. He looks so damn serious that it takes my breath away. "I'm not easy to be around."

"Never."

"I have no idea what my life will be like. If this spell will work, or if I'll have to live a life I never imagined before all of this. One behind walls at all times. Or one running forever."

"I don't care, as long as we're together," he whispers, then leans down and kisses me. *Hard.* Hard enough that everything around me fades away.

And then when he breaks our kiss, his eyes stay closed

for a long minute before those green pools open once more, and he smiles down at me. "Is that okay with you?"

"Right now it is," I tell him, smiling.

He leans down and kisses me again. And again. Each kiss lasts longer than the one before it, until his tongue darts into my mouth, and his hand digs into the back of my hair, angling me for easier access. The world sweeps away, and there's nothing except him and me. His big, hard body against me. Our hearts beating in rhythm. He's holding me like I'm something important and fragile.

His lips break from mine, and he trails his lips down my throat while one of his hands slides down my body, making goosebumps erupt on my flesh, and I realize I'm panting. Wanting more. *Needing* Bash more than air.

I think of all the many moments in my life when I wanted him. When we'd wrestle. When he'd best me in a fight and let that smug little smile of his blossom on his lips. I even think of us when he picked me up to take me to the guild, how I'd tried to attack him in the hotel, how he'd pinned me underneath him and kept my underwear as his prize.

The memories are strangely a turn-on. It amazes me to think that Bash and I have never actually slept together, even though the chemistry between us is like electricity, always crackling between us. But he and I have been walking this tightrope for too long. I'm tired of it. I just want him now, and I know he wants me. So why not?

"B-Bash," I pant his name.

"*Humm*?" he murmurs against my skin.

"I think we should sleep together tonight."

He freezes and draws back, his expression surprised. "Really?"

I nod. "I don't want to wait any longer."

He grins and picks me up by my ass, and my legs naturally wrap around his waist. He starts to carry us to the bed when I notice Rian watching us, hunger in his eyes.

"Rian!" I gasp, remembering we're not alone.

Rian flashes his fangs. "Don't mind me. I think I'll enjoy watching."

My breath comes in and out faster. "You're sure?"

He nods, looking *entirely* sure.

Bash switches directions, then lays me down on the bed from the side, probably to give Rian a better angle, which excites me in the strangest way. Then, he reaches down and pulls my shirt off, followed by my pants. His movements are jerky. His eyes have darkened with desire. It's incredible watching how badly he seems to want me naked. His hands are practically shaking.

And I feel the same way.

But when he reaches for my bra, he hesitates, then reaches for his shirt instead. He tugs it off slowly, displaying a wealth of muscles on his belly, then his chest, and then his big arms as he throws his shirt to the side. He looks so big and perfect standing over me as he reaches for the button on his pants and undoes it before yanking his zipper down and removing his pants, instantly showing his big erection beneath his boxers.

When he stands to his full height again, his gaze is hooded as he stares down at me. And it occurs to me that neither of us has really seen the other one naked before. Not like this. And it feels oddly vulnerable, like I'm letting him see a piece of my soul that I keep only to myself.

Yet...it feels right.

He leans over me on his elbow, bringing our faces inches from each other. But while I look at his mouth, expecting a kiss, he doesn't give me one. Instead, his hand moves down the center of my body, from my throat, down the valley of my breasts, and then all the way to the edge of my underwear.

His touch sends tingles spreading over my body, and I'm practically holding my breath, waiting for whatever he might do next. Luckily, he doesn't make me wait long. He slowly pushes beneath my underwear, parts me, and starts to stroke me.

I gasp and grasp his wrist, but he just continues to stroke me gently, as if he knows this is exactly what I need. My body twitches as my nerves are overwhelmed with desire. It's like my nerves are guitar strings, and he's playing them just right.

His mouth slips down as he continues to stroke my body, and my skin feels ridiculously sensitive as he kisses the tops of my breasts, then uses his lips to push aside my bra before sucking on my nipple.

It's too much. Overwhelming. *Bash* is sucking on my nipple. *Bash* is touching my pussy. *How the hell is this my life now?*

My head falls to the side, and I see Rian. He's pushed down his pants and boxers. His long, thick dick is in his hand as he strokes himself slowly, watching Bash touch me.

My body jerks again, and desire races through me. *How the hell is it this hot to watch Rian getting off to Bash touching me?* A million pictures swim through my mind about what a future with three romantic partners might look like. And, strangely, every picture is a good one.

I can do this. Fuck, I might want to do this every day for the rest of my life.

Bash moves to my other breast, and my eyes close. I can practically feel Rian stroking himself still. And the image allows me to slip away for a moment as I become nothing but nerves. Nothing but desire.

And then my bra snaps open, and my eyes do too. I barely have time to react before Bash is tearing my underwear off. He's panting, and I can almost feel the demon part of him roaring to life. He tears down his boxers, then stands in front of me, every inch of him explaining his arrogance.

Fuck. Of course Bash has a giant cock.

He grabs me by the thighs and pulls me further down the side of the bed so that my ass is practically hanging off. He pushes himself between my thighs, and I shudder as the tip of his cock parts my folds. For a minute he just rubs himself around in my juices, then, suddenly, presses into my core.

"Bash! Fucking hell!" I cry out.

He doesn't hesitate. He doesn't slow. He just begins to fuck me like his life depends on making me orgasm, and as lighting strikes of pleasure crash into me over and over again, I'm screaming his name, moving so that we thrust together at the same moment. Stars dance before my vision with each powerful stroke of his dick.

As my orgasm starts to build and build, I dig my nails into his back, and he growls my name. His rhythm increases, as does the power of his strokes, and I'm holding my breath as my head swings to the side.

Rian is standing, stroking himself in a fury of movement. His teeth suddenly clench together. His eyes darken, and I know what's about to happen.

And it does.

I watch him come, his seed exploding from his tip as he continues to work the white substance over his length. It goes and goes, my name slipping from his lips as he clenches himself tightly. And it's that erotic sight that finally pushes me over the edge.

My orgasm hits me like a ton of glorious bricks. I stop screaming, stop saying anything, as the pleasure rocks my body. Rocks my mind.

Which is exactly when I feel Bash come too. He shudders on top of me, saying my name almost like a prayer as his seed fills my body. It's incredible, the feeling of him inside of me. Of knowing that he's mine, *all* mine, and that I'll never lose him again.

Once upon a time, we were best friends, then enemies, and now...lovers. Not just lovers but two people who truly love each other. And that's magical. Even if that might sound cheesy, I don't care. Because it's true.

And I love it.

He collapses on top of me, us both panting. Lost in the aftermath of our lovemaking. Wanting to make this moment last for as long as possible.

After a few minutes, he kisses the side of my neck and whispers in my ear, "Ares still needs my help tonight. But for a little while, I just want to hold you, if that's okay."

I nod, and Bash cleans us up, then tugs me into the center of the bed. Rian comes out of the bathroom, having cleaned himself up too. We all lay down together, me in the center of them, and Bash says, "You'll stay with her all night?"

"I will," Rian promises, his voice soft and sweet.

Bash releases a slow breath, then kisses me again.

And it's weird, but I feel really damn loved.

And really damn lucky.

10

MERCY

It's late when I wake up, sweating and shaking. I'd had a nightmare about my phoenix mom being chained to a chair beneath this castle. She was screaming and screaming for me to save her, but no matter how hard I tried to reach her, she only got further away.

I shift a little and realize that Rian is still wrapped around me. I reach for Bash, but find that side of the bed cold and empty. For a moment my heart pangs, but then I remember how he'd kissed me goodbye, apologized, and tucked me in before leaving the night before. He might not be here right now, but he hadn't just disappeared on me after our night tonight.

Who would have thought I'd ever wake up smiling and thinking of Bash? Then my smile fades as my dream presses back into my mind.

Gently, I remove Rian's arm from around my waist and climb out of bed. I'm already getting dressed and putting on my daggers before I fully understand what I'm doing. No, I won't be freeing the prisoners tonight, no matter how much

I want to, but neither can I keep laying in a bed sleeping when people were going through hell so close to me.

Glancing back one more time at Rian, I can't help but smile. Everyone around here might see him as some badass vampire prince, but I'd always see him in another light. Even if instead of marrying him I just run away one day, accepting a life where I would always be running, but at least be free to make my own choices.

Not that I want to think about a life without my men at my side.

I look away from him, then slip down the hall. I have no clue where I'm going except that I'm headed outside. Something about this place or these people made me feel...imprisoned in a way I can't explain. Like instead of seeing myself as some wealthy guest here, I feel like the people in cages. I just don't have bars on my prison cell.

Which is stupid. No one is forcing me to stay here. And I feel like an ass even relating to the blood slaves. What they've been through, I can only imagine.

Guards patrol everywhere, but I stretch out my senses and do my best to avoid being seen by all of them. I slip into a library on the bottom floor, find a window, and crawl out. More guards patrol the outside of the castle, but I slip past them too. I'm about to just run like hell for the trees when I spot the stables nearly tucked out of view to one side of the house. The stables, where Ares's father spends most of his time. And just beyond that, I know, is the home Ares grew up in. A little cottage nestled near the stables and the trees.

I've never seen it, but Ares has told me so many stories about the stables and his home over the years that I feel like I have.

Sensing a guard rounding the corner, I slip into the shadows, force my breathing and heartbeat to slow even quieter, and then wait for him to pass. When I'm in the clear, I dart across the lawn to the stables and slip inside.

Instantly, I'm hit with the smell of large animals and hay. I inhale slowly. I've always liked the scent of a clean stable, even as a kid. Henry and I would brush the horses together and talk about how I could improve and be in better shape for the guild. Sometimes, I'd climb into the loft in our stable, lay in the hay, and just relax. There were few times in my life that I ever felt that safe.

As I stare at this stable, which is admittedly larger than mine back home, I see a similar loft to the one I hid in as a kid. I'm not even thinking when I climb up into it and then lay down in the hay with a sigh. I just look out over the stable and feel a wealth of emotions sweeping over me. Tears prick my eyes, but I don't cry. I just try to enjoy the moment.

Before too much longer, I'll have to figure out how to handle my father and the other phoenixes, how to help my brother, and how to deal with a vampire prince wanting to marry me to keep me safe.

But not now. Not tonight.

My eyes flutter closed. I know it's stupid, but it almost feels like Henry is here with me, telling me everything will be okay. And then, my eyes flash back open. *Is it strange that I lost my parents and yet all I seem to be able to focus on is Henry?* I don't know. Loss is...complicated.

The door to the barn opens faster and wider than when I'd opened it, and a small groan comes from the hinges. I glance down in shock to see Ares and his father walking in together. They're both still dressed like they were at dinner, which tells me that whatever they've been up to, they haven't gone to sleep yet. Ares pauses at the door to the barn, glances out, then closes it slowly behind him.

"So, what did you want to talk to me about that you couldn't say in front of the king?"

His dad throws him a brush for the horses, which he catches with ease, and then his father leads a horse out of a stall and they begin to brush it together, like they've done this same thing a thousand times before. "There's a lot to discuss, actually."

Ares says nothing. No surprise there. He just waits.

"I was wondering about how you felt about Prince Drakkar setting his sights on Mercy. I know you've been in love with her from the first time you saw her."

I hold my breath. *In love with me?* Yeah, he is now. *But had he really always been and I just hadn't noticed?*

No. No way.

"It's complicated," Ares says. He hesitates, and then pushes on. "I know that you always had a picture in your mind about who I would end up with. Someone like mom, I think, even though you didn't say it. And from what I know of my mom, she's about as opposite from Mercy as she can be."

"We don't need to talk about her." His father's voice is harsh, almost unkind in a way I've never heard it before.

Ares releases a slow breath. "I ran into members of Pack Forgotten. Your old packmates."

His father's hand drops from the horse and he actually staggers back a couple of steps, his face pale. "What happened?"

"They attacked me. And Mercy." His father opens his mouth, but Ares pushes forward. "I also learned what happened to mom and why you were thrown out and your ability to shift taken away."

"No." His father sounds like he's talking to himself. "I never wanted you to know."

"What that man did to mom...that was horrible. And everything you did was completely justified. I want you to know that. And I also want you to know that after meeting the pack members, I'm glad I'm not a part of that pack. I'm glad you got us out and gave us the life you did."

His father's gaze moves to his son, and then it slowly drifts back to the horse as he begins brushing its body once more. He doesn't say anything for so long that I wonder if they're done talking, if this is how they simply are together, but then his dad says, "I'm sorry you had to go through that, but I'm glad you're okay."

"I'm more than okay. I'm glad to know what happened. It feels like it makes it easier to move on...to look at my future with Mercy with hope."

His dad scoffs. "Prince Drakkar is planning on marrying Mercy. You'll have to find a way to let her go."

Ares shakes his head. "You don't understand. We agreed that Rian should marry her, but Bash and I have no intention of dropping our claim on her. If she is open to it, the four of us would be in a relationship together."

The older man shakes his head. "We're not fae or berserkers. We don't typically have more than one partner."

"Well, we will." Ares sounds so damned confident. "No matter what happens, I'll never lose Mercy or Bash or Rian. We've become our own kind of family, and I love them more than anyone could imagine."

I swear I can see a million emotions racing across his father's face before he settles on one. Maybe...acceptance? "I don't know if that's the path I would have picked for you," his dad gives a little shrug, "but I guess I should just be glad you found love."

Ares gives one of his rare smiles. "You should be. You will be. You'll see. I know you always thought Mercy would break my heart, but she won't. With her, with them, I'm happy. And I don't care about anything else."

Damn it. Here I am thinking about whether I'm going to run away from all of this, and Ares goes and says something like that. Something to remind me that the world doesn't revolve around me, and I need to pull my head out of my ass.

His dad gives a slow nod, then stops brushing the horse. "Speaking of that." He clears his throat. "There's been something I've been meaning to tell you for a long time, but it never seemed like the right time, if that makes sense."

Ares's brows draw together in that way that says he's worried but is trying really hard to keep it to himself, which I get. Whatever his dad is leading up to, it must be a doozy.

His dad clears his throat once more, starts brushing the horse again, then stops. "The thing is...well...love is complicated...and, uh, sometimes, people love. Sometimes they don't. Sometimes their choices surprise people and, uh, even themselves."

Ares is staring, hard.

"I'm in love," his father blurts out.

And Ares smiles. Not one of his small smiles but one that lights up his whole face. "That's wonderful! Why didn't you tell me sooner? You know how much I want you to be happy."

"It's just...complicated," he says, watching his son closely.

"Mercy is complicated, but she's right for me," Ares tells him with a little shrug that makes my heart melt. Even though I don't know how I feel about being called *complicated*. The thing is, he isn't wrong.

His dad moves around the horse, reaches out, and squeezes his son's shoulder, looking him square in the eye. "The person I love is, well, King Drakkar."

Mercy's Rise

My jaw drops open. *Ares's dad and Rian's dad? They're...together?*

Ares takes a few steps back, then collapses onto a bale of hay. "King Drakkar?"

His dad nods, looking pale.

"And does he love you back?"

His dad nods once more.

"And how long have you been together?"

His dad runs a hand through his hair. "At first, it was more of a friendship, a bond, but over the years, especially since you boys left, it changed. And one night, he admitted his feelings for me, and I admitted mine for him. In public, we keep a professional relationship, but in private, we've been together for years. One of the main reasons he wants the prince to take over the throne and for us to move to a private place is because he wants us to enjoy the rest of our lives together without being under a microscope. Without having to constantly worry that someone will hurt me to get to him. He doesn't care if people know he's gay. I'm just the first person, other than his son, that he wants to protect from the harsh world he's a part of. And with the recent increase in attempts on his life, he doesn't like the idea that my job is to step in front of a bullet for him, when his instinct is to do the same for me."

Ares leans back, stares at the floor for a minute, then meets his father's nervous gaze. "I guess...I'm happy then. If you're happy. Because that's all I've ever wanted for you."

My amazing shifter stands. The two awkwardly shake hands, and then he pulls his dad into a hug, and they're both grinning and clinging to each other.

"I missed you so much," his dad says.

"I missed you too."

Their hug lasts for a long minute before Ares pats his

dad on the back. They return the horse to its stable, then head out, chatting in low voices. For some reason, I'm smiling. Okay, so his dad didn't want us to be together, no surprise there. But we have his blessing in a weird way now, and I know this will take a huge weight off of Ares's shoulders to know his dad has found love. That he isn't as lonely as Ares thought he was.

I sigh and inhale the scent of more hay. Some of the tension in my muscles eased. Tension I didn't even know had been there. But something is still wrong.

Closing my eyes, I search for what might be upsetting me so much. I've never been very good at figuring out my own feelings, or self-reflecting. I usually just ace the whole piling on emotional baggage until I explode in an unhealthy way thing, so trying to figure out my feelings is new to me.

And then, it hits me. And it's so damn obvious I want to smack myself.

Instead, I sneak back into the house. The coronation, apparently, will take place in a few days' time. Before then, there is something important I need to do.

Going back through the house, I sneak down the stairs, unlock the entrance to the basement, and duck into the space with all the blood slaves. No one else is down here, no one but the slaves, but I still try to stay quiet. I go to each of their cells, kneel down, and explain my plan. They all immediately perk up, and by the time I've visited each cell, I have a good feeling my plan will work.

These people...they won't be prisoners for much longer. They'll get free, Rian's name will be in the clear, and no one will even think to glance in my direction.

I just hope everything goes as planned.

11

*B*ASH

It's been a long-ass week. No matter how many forces we send to the twelve families, the phoenixes continue to attack, continue to kill and destroy. I'd heard they were also working with a variety of supernaturals, mostly hired thugs, and essentially sending them out first to deal the worst of the blows. Bodies are piling up, on our side and theirs.

People are not happy. They've been reaching out to their leaders, including the vampire king, asking for a solution to the angry phoenixes and their army of thugs. And, apparently, a solution is in the works, but that's all I've heard.

Although I suspect it'll be a violent solution.

Mercy has been working her hardest to try to get the phoenixes to communicate with her, but every attempt has been met with silence. She's pleaded with her father. Begged him. But she hears nothing in response, except the one messenger's head that was returned to us in a box.

I can see it in her eyes every day when we learn about the next family's attack: Mercy's losing faith. She wants to believe that after all her kind has been through, they're just trying to do the right thing the wrong way, that they can be reasoned with, but she's now the only person who still believes that.

The rest of us...we know it's time for more drastic measures.

Rian comes into the library, where we've set up our "station" to handle the phoenix issue. He sees me slumped over the desk, hand buried in my hair, and gives me a sympathetic look. "Long night?"

"Oh, gosh, is it morning already?" I groan and wince at the unopened curtains.

A moment later, Rian is pulling them back, and this time I groan louder and shield my eyes from the bright morning sunlight. Rian is rested, dressed for the new day, and screaming with energy. I'd probably get a little stabby with him if he hadn't been the one to stay up the night before.

"Any news?" he asks.

I shake my head. "No new attack reported. Yet. But it's still early."

He nods and sits down in the chair across from me and the big desk. "How's Mercy holding up?"

"She stayed until pretty late last night going over everything. I think she's trying to find some explanation, outside of a desire for blood and revenge, for what is motivating the phoenixes." I sigh. "It's weird. Her MO is to look for the worst in most people, but with these phoenixes, it's like she has blinders on."

Rian lifts a brow. "Is it really any surprise that a woman treated like shit by the only family she ever knew desperately wants to see something good in her second, and only, chance at another family?"

"We're her family," I blurt out, then feel a bit stupid. Of course Rian knows we're a family.

His eyes widen, but then he nods. "Maybe we just need to remind her of that."

He's probably right. "And the plans for the coronation?"

Now I see his nervousness. It's in the way he crosses his arms over his chest and the way he bounces his legs "It is what it is."

"That bad?"

He doesn't even laugh. "I will be king in a couple of days, whether I want to be or not."

To some people, he might sound spoiled, or even like an asshole, but I don't blame him one bit. I wouldn't take the vampire crown if it was thrown at me. If Rian thought his life was micromanaged before, if he was worried about attempts against his life before, it'll be nothing compared to what he'll experience once he's king.

"Your father seems pretty happy about it..."

Rian gives a short nod. "He confided in me about his relationship with Ares's father, and, apparently, Ares was told too. As much as I don't want to do this, my father has worn the crown for a long time. It only makes sense that he wants to be done with it, to enjoy the remainder of his long life."

"It must make this pill a little easier to swallow."

"It does." Rian rubs the back of his neck. "But his plans to handle the phoenixes before he steps down is making everything infinitely harder. I don't think he believes I have the balls to handle this situation the way it needs to be, and I might agree."

"What does he plan to do?" I ask, frowning.

Rian opens his mouth but the door opens, stopping him. Mercy comes into the room wearing a black tank top and dark jeans, which both look amazing on her. All exhaustion fades away, and I can't seem to take my eyes off of her. Not *any* part of her. Not the way her bright blue eyes focus on us with such intelligence, not the way her long hair swings behind her in a ponytail as she walks, or the incredible way her hips move as she comes toward us.

"Fuck, Mercy," I groan her name.

She lifts a brow, comes around the desk, and is suddenly in my lap. "Rough night?" she purrs, then wiggles in my lap.

"Fuck," I manage again, then pull her down and kiss her so hard and fast that it takes my breath away. When she breaks our kiss, we're both panting, and I'm hoping she's as aroused as I am. Something about seeing her after a rough night just makes me want to bury myself in her and forget all about the real world.

"Morning."

I turn my head and realize Ares has come in. He looks a little embarrassed, or maybe turned on, as he looks at us. Either way, his cheeks are flushed.

"You realize I have three men in my life and yet none of you slept with me last night," Mercy says.

"Did you miss us?" Rian asks, his voice low and aroused.

Oh, hell. I hope this is going where I think it's going.

"I *really* missed you guys," Mercy says, then flutters her lashes.

Rian gives her a look, then gets up and goes to the door, locking it. "How about you show us just how much you missed us?"

She laughs. "I'm not some girl in a porno. You guys show me how much you missed *me*."

I exchange a look with Rian, then with Ares. We're all suddenly grinning. *She wants us to show her how much we missed her? Done.* But she might regret her fast mouth this early in the morning.

Standing, I sweep her into my arms, then set her on my

chair. She looks disappointed as I walk away from her, and then Rian goes to his music player and mumbles the song he wants. A minute later, I'm Too Sexy starts to play. He turns up the volume so that it's blaring, and then we all line up in front of Mercy, right behind the chairs.

Her brows are so high they're lost in her hair. "What the hell is this?"

And then, we start to dance, using all our best moves. Her jaw drops as we start to take off our shirts. Rian unbuttons his slowly, while I pull my shirt off and fling it at her. Ares drops his onto the floor, his cheeks pink, but his hips moving like he dirty dances for women every day.

Then we're working on our pants, swinging our hips, shaking our asses, making every proud stripper even prouder with our "sexy" moves. Mercy finally manages to close her mouth, but she still looks shocked rather than aroused. Until Ares drops his pants, kicking them and his shoes off. I'm oddly proud when I see him erect as hell in his grey boxer briefs. And he doesn't stop there; he's thrusting toward her like this is how he makes his money every damn day. Rian launches his pants across the room, leaving nothing but his dark blue boxer briefs. He's already aroused too, but he's shaking his hands above his head in a way that has me laughing, even when I take off my own pants and shoes, showing off my black boxers.

Mercy's hungry gaze sweeps over us all and she says, "I should make fun of you guys more."

In answer to her words, I circle around the desk, put one foot on the top of the desk, then start thrusting my erection in front of her face. Her eyes go wide, and then she's laughing. Ares and Rian manage to position themselves around her, and then we're all thrusting in her face. I happen to glance up and make eye contact with a gardener, who looks horrified, before he scatters away.

Setting my leg down, I make it to the window and draw the curtains closed while the next song, Hot In Here, plays. This time, I move close to Mercy and slowly work my boxers down until my cock comes exploding out of my clothes, and then I drop my boxers onto the floor. I proceed to "ride" my underwear around the desk, and then Rian sets his foot back down on the floor and drops his boxers in one quick move, followed by swinging his dick around in circles while she stares at him with wide eyes.

At last, Ares moves away from her desk and drops his boxer briefs, then does a funny little dance while she laughs. And then, we're all naked, and she's grinning at us. But if she thought this was all just a fun show for her benefit, she's about to find out otherwise.

"We showed you ours," I tell her.

She raises a brow. "And so, you want to see mine?"

We all nod.

She stands, looking oddly smug. "The thing is, if I get naked, I have a feeling we're all going to fuck."

"Yup!" Ares exclaims.

She looks even smugger. "And even though I've had three guys at once before..."

I feel anger wash over me. Maybe not anger, but jealousy, and I'm about ready to track down anyone Mercy has ever slept with and kill them. Luckily for me, Rian speaks before I can. "We don't need to know about that, because it's nothing like what we're going to do to you."

"Really?" She crosses her arms over her chest. "And how will it be different with the three of you?"

The red in Rian's eyes brightens and his fangs elongate, showing just how close to the edge he already is. But he circles behind her, then whispers, loud enough for us to hear, "Have you ever had two men in your ass at the same time?" Before she can answer, he presses up against her from behind and grabs one of her breasts lightly, leaning and nibbling gently on her neck.

She shudders so hard that we all see her. "No."

"Do you want to feel it? Because I swear to God, you'll never regret it."

"So, two cocks in my ass, that's how this will be different?" she asks, but she sounds out of breath.

"And all three of us love you," Ares sputters out.

Rian gives him a look, as if to remind him we're trying to fuck our beautiful woman, and make it hot, not gush about our feelings. Mercy might know how we feel, but she's not the type of woman who wants to hear about feelings and emotions more than she has to, and the bashful look on Ares's face says he might have realized that.

"So," Mercy draws out the word. "Love and two cocks in my ass? Okay then, let's see if this really does rock my world."

Rian doesn't need to hear anything else; he's yanking off her shirt within seconds. Ares and I come around the desk and start working on her pants and boots while Rian removes her bra. For some reason, my heart is racing. It's not like we haven't shared a woman before, but Mercy isn't just any woman. She's *our* woman. This needs to be good for her. It's our first real opportunity to show her that the four of us can really have a romantic relationship together and that maybe, just maybe, our plan to have her marry Rian for protection and stay with all of us will work.

But all of those careful, smart plans go out the window when she's suddenly standing in front of us naked.

My mouth goes dry. I stare at her on her knees, shocked

by the way heat seems to shoot straight through me. My cock bobs as if in agreement, and before I know what I'm doing, I clear the desk, throwing everything on it onto the floor. A second later, I toss her onto the desk, spread her thighs, and press my mouth to her hot core. She gasps, and her hand digs into my hair as I press my lips against her over and over, soft kisses, while she watches me with eyes filled with desire.

Ares moves to one side of the desk and Rian to the other. Ares kisses her soft lips, while Rian takes hold of her breasts. Her eyes close and her head rolls back, and then I relax, knowing my woman's every need is being met as I focus on my delicious task at hand.

Mercy smells like heaven, sweeter than anyone could ever imagine, and as I part her, I begin to slowly lick her wet folds, marveling at her taste, which is just as sweet as her smell. Her body jerks around me, and her hand pulls my head closer, which is all I need to know to tell me she's liking it. And then I forget everything. Everything except this woman.

I'm not just licking her or kissing her, I'm working my tongue through her folds to build her desire, then flicking her clit with my tongue at the right moments to hear her gasp in surprise. Then, when I'm drowning in the evidence of her desire, I bring my fingers into it too. I press two slowly into her pussy, enjoying the incredible sensation of her body holding me tightly, oh so fucking tightly. I hear the sounds of her body growing wetter and wetter and add a third finger, then a fourth.

She is shaking so much that I know she's fighting her orgasm, which I know is the perfect moment. So, I look up, meeting Rian's and Ares's gazes. I use my hands to push her legs up higher, and then they each take a leg, holding them up, and parting them to give me an incredible amount of access to everything I need.

Drawing my fingers out of her pussy, I choose one and slowly press it into her ass. She tenses for a moment, so I freeze and focus back on licking her sweet core until she slowly relaxes. Then, I press my finger deeper and deeper into her body, letting her grow used to me with each second that passes. When I'm sure she's ready for it, I start to thrust my finger slowly in and out while she thrashes and moans. Ares's mouth captures her sounds, but only a little. I can still enjoy every little noise she makes that tells me she's enjoying what I'm doing.

Rian has moved to sucking her breasts, plucking them, biting them gently. All the things we know our woman likes, and I watch her being touched and enjoyed by my friends, while still trying to keep control of my desires. I sure as hell don't plan to explode right here and give any of them the satisfaction of knowing I couldn't keep control.

I add another finger. And another. And another. Slowly. Building her desire. Feeling when it's too much and slowing. Doing everything I can to prepare our woman, but not hurt her.

At last, Rian catches my gaze and gives a little nod. *Fuck, he's right. It's time.* None of us are going to last much longer, and this is supposed to be perfect. Proof to our women that our relationship is right, just the way it is.

I pull my fingers out of her incredible ass and draw my mouth away from her pussy. She gives a little whimper as we all shift, and then I say, "I'll lift her. Ares, get on the desk."

He does as he's told while I lift her, then Rian takes her from me and places her on top of Ares. Our wolf shifter looks pleased as hell as she wiggles on top of him, shifts, grabs his cock, and slowly sinks down onto it.

This time, he's groaning, throwing back his head like this is the best moment of his life. And I don't blame him one bit. There's nothing better than our sweet Mercy's pussy, except maybe her ass. I guess I'll know which I prefer soon.

"First or second?" I ask Rian.

He studies her ass for a moment, then groans the word, "First," before climbing on top of her on the desk.

I sit back in the office chair for a moment, reaching down and grasping my cock and stroking slowly. Ares is kissing our woman again, while Rian fondles her breasts from behind. I know they're wanting to be sure she's ready, but I can tell she is. Yet, I take deep breaths, telling myself to keep it together for just a little longer.

And, sure enough, my patience pays off. Rian releases one of her breasts, reaches between them, and grabs his cock, then slowly angles it into her ass while I'm almost jumping out of my chair, cock in hand. I have to start repeating guild rules to keep from exploding right then and there as he squeezes himself inside of her.

But I keep control, and then get to watch while the two men work together to slowly start fucking her. Maybe I should be jealous, but I'm not. I know what's coming next, and I can just imagine how good it'll feel. Still, when the men pause and look back at me, I scramble toward the desk, level my cock at her ass, then slowly push it in beside Rian's cock.

Mercy cries out, so I pause, and then she shouts, "Don't stop!" like I'm an idiot.

So, I don't. I keep squeezing in, even when it seems impossible that me and the big vampire will both fit into our tiny woman. But none of us stop. We work together, moving carefully until I come to my hilt.

Once there, I stop for a minute. Ares kisses Mercy again,

and Rian sweeps her hair to one side and slides his fangs into her throat. It's erotic as hell to watch, but then we all begin to move together, thrusting in and out of her while she pants, then begins to moan, and finally breaks her mouth from Ares's to murmur words that make no sense.

Which is the moment we pick up the pace.

The world fades away. Everything fades away except Mercy and her tight ass. My cock swells larger and larger. Both rubbing against Rian's and squeezing into Mercy's body make for such an incredible combination that stars actually explode in front of my vision, and then I'm coming, shouting her name, working myself so hard and fast that I'm barely aware when Mercy's body tightens and she comes screaming, slamming into her orgasm as my friends come too. We're all moving together, riding the waves of our orgasms, and it's like nothing I ever imagined. It's better than anything else we've done.

Ever.

It's several long moments before I collapse, as do they all, and then we're just a tangled pile of naked bodies, panting, sweaty, and pleased as fuck.

And we stay like that for a while. Strangely content until Mercy begins to shift a bit, and I release a slow breath, realizing that this too has to end.

"What do you think?" Ares murmurs, sweeping the hair away from Mercy's face.

She takes too long to answer, but her panting is almost its own answer. "That was...incredible."

"Better than your other experiences?" Rian asks, his voice edged with jealousy.

"Much better," she almost moans.

I pull out of her, and then everyone is moving around. Rian kisses our Mercy, as does Ares, and I help her get cleaned up and dressed before getting myself ready. It feels like this incredible moment where all our problems are gone. Where there's nothing but us.

And then, the phone rings.

Rian sighs and shoves his foot into his shoe, completing his outfit, before answering, "Hello."

In an instant, his face changes. "Okay."

"What's wrong?" Mercy mouths, and suddenly all the tension of the real world is back.

Damn it.

Rian lifts his head from the receiver and looks at me. "Your family was attacked last night."

I reach for the phone without thinking, my heart racing. "Hello?"

To my relief, it's my mother. "We were attacked by those damned phoenixes," she says, the last word sobbed.

"Is everyone okay?"

She's crying softly, struggling through her words. "We lost a lot of good men, but your stepfather, your brothers, and I, we're all okay. Because of your instructions, we knew what to expect. I think if they'd have caught us by surprise..." Another sob.

"Do you want me to come home?"

My mom never wants me to come home. She loves me, but she has her hands full with my siblings. Pushing me toward becoming an assassin was one of the many ways she tried to give us all things to do, so we wouldn't all just grow up to be spoiled children ready to take our parents' money. But that was sort of expected in a family with six sons, even if it hurt sometimes.

"No," my mother says. "You'll do more good there in stopping those monsters, permanently."

We talk for a little longer while she goes over the

damages and losses of life, and then her worries that they'll be attacked again, before my stepfather comes onto the phone and says she needs to rest. I thank him for taking care of her, then set down the phone.

Everyone is looking at me. "My family is okay."

There's a collective sigh of relief.

"But they're worried the phoenixes will come back."

"If they'd just talk to me!" Mercy explodes. "I could stop this, I know I could."

"Unfortunately," Rian says, avoiding her gaze, "I think we've run out of time."

"What does that mean?" she asks.

Rian looks at me. All of us already know, even though no one outside of this castle knows.

"My father, he's come up with a plan," Rian tells her gravely.

Her face falls. "What kind of plan?"

I know he wants to tell her gently, but there's no gentle way to say this. "He thinks he's found a way to kill the phoenixes, for good. All of them."

"No!" She's shaking her head, backing away from us. "We can't just kill all of them!"

"We're out of options," Rian tells her, reaching out for her.

"How? How is he going to do it?" She sounds desperate.

Ares and I don't know yet, but we got the sense that it'll be awful. Not that we should say that.

We all exchange another look, but it's Rian who speaks. "I'm not allowed to say."

Her eyes flash with rage. "So I'm supposed to trust you with my heart and body, but you don't have to trust me with important information?"

"It's not like that," I say.

"It is!" she says, whirling on me. "And if I just went to their castle and spoke to them, I know--"

"No!" we all shout at the same time.

She glares at all of us. "Fuck you!" And then, she storms out.

"Damn it," I mutter, collapsing into a chair.

My parents were attacked. My home was attacked. We finally got to share Mercy, and it's all been overshadowed by the shit with the phoenixes.

"She's not going to do anything stupid, is she?" Ares asks.

Rian snorts. "Of course she is. We just have to be there to protect her."

He's right. But still, I replay the look on her face and hate the ache in my chest.

12

M<small>ERCY</small>

It's late when I slip out of the mansion, weaving my way through shadows until I can fully hide in the trees. Once there, I pause, breathing hard and looking back in the direction I'd come from. No one is there, watching me, chasing me. Nothing. It seems I got away without being spotted. Which is normally a good thing, but somehow, I feel strange. *Guilty, maybe?*

Which is stupid. This is the right decision for me, for the phoenixes, for all the families. So why does it feel like I'm betraying the men I love?

Because you know they'd stop you from doing this, tell you it's dangerous, and inevitably change your mind about trying to handle this yourself. Damn it. The treacherous thought ticks me off because it's right.

Still, I turn away from the castle and continue slipping between the shadows of the trees, hesitating when guards cross my path, then pushing on until I reach the fence around the castle. Looking up at the high wall, I continue slipping along it until I find a branch hanging low enough and close enough that I can use it to get to the other side of the fence.

Taking a deep breath, I climb into the tree and then do exactly that, calculating as I go how far away the car will be hidden in the trees on the other side. Hopefully, at least.

When I jump down on the other side, it takes me a little while to get my bearings before I make my way closer to the road leading to the castle and then use it as a guide to find the car hidden away in the woods. I'd paid a pretty penny to have it delivered here by a sketchy fellow I had contacts through, and I would tear him a new one if he was lying about getting it here.

I walk along the side of the road, just out of sight, feeling my frustration rising. This is it. My one chance to talk to my people. Tomorrow is the coronation. Important guests are already coming in droves, and I know for sure I won't be able to slip out after the coronation. So, this is really it.

If the whispers I'd heard were true, in the next few days the king will be launching an attack on the phoenixes that can actually kill all of them in some mysterious way that sounds horrifying, although I'm still not sure what it is yet. Then, there will be no going back. I'll have stood by and allowed every last one of my kind to be murdered.

Whether they deserve it or not, the idea makes me sick.

So, tonight, I will try to reason with them before more damage is done. Before more people die. The others might think the phoenixes are so blinded by their desire for revenge that they won't listen, but I don't believe that for one minute. I honestly wonder if only one person among the phoenixes, or a small group, is receiving the messages and not responding. Or if it is that all of them are just forgetting that there's more to life than this.

I really don't know. I've run through every possibility in my mind.

But all I can hope is that if I can see them, face-to-face, everything will change. My father will hear my words, know that they're true, and we'll be able to convince the others. Maybe just seeing his daughter will be enough for him to remember there's more to life than just death and revenge. *Something* will click. There simply has to be a way to stop this war without the extinction of my people. *Again.*

And yet, I can't find the damned car.

I'm still trying to remain quiet and move quickly, so it ticks me off when I have to stop, lean against a tree, and stretch out my senses in a deeper way. At first, my frustration blocks my senses, and then my heartbeat slows, along with my breathing, and it's like the world around me comes alive in a new and different way. I can almost sense every tree around me. Every creature's heartbeat. Even the guards who walk along the walls, on both sides. But if I thought this would help me find the mysterious car, I was wrong.

Half a second later, I freeze. Maybe there's no car, but there *is* something in the woods now. It appeared almost out of thin air. Something big, that burns hotter than a fire, standing between me and the castle. It instantly begins to move in my direction, faster than most creatures can go.

My eyes flash open. *Hellhound.*

A blind panic fills me, and I start to run in the opposite direction. This was such a stupid decision. I'm a fucking moron. I knew that people were aware of my existence. I knew they'd sent hellhounds after me before. Just because things with those monstrous creatures have been quiet since coming to the castle, that doesn't mean the people who wanted to use me as a blood source have given up, and thinking otherwise is going to get me killed.

I can't outrun the creature behind me. I can't fight it. One bite from its massive mouth, and it'll lock onto me and drag me, teleport me, to whatever master it serves, and I'll never be free again.

No one will hear me scream. My men will never know what happened to me. I'll simply vanish into the night.

So many times in my life I thought I understood fear, understood true terror. But this is so far beyond anything I've ever felt before, and I realize that I've developed a new phobia. Of dying, lost and forgotten.

The hellhound is gaining on me. No matter how fast I run, I can sense it drawing closer. I even imagine its breath on my neck. My feet stumble on a root, and I hit my knees before quickly leaping back to my feet and continuing to run, even though I can't slow my heartbeat or my breathing. I just keep pushing myself harder and harder, praying for a miracle.

It's close. Close enough that when I hear it howl, it sends a shiver rolling down my spine.

It'll be on me in moments.

And then, up ahead, I see something flash in the darkness. Without knowing what I'm doing, I adjust my direction toward the flash of light. Which is when I realize the light is coming from the moon's rays hitting a car hidden by branches.

My legs pump harder. I dive at the car, throw open the door, and climb in. Instantly, I'm reaching under the seat. That's where he'd said the keys were, but my hands come up empty. And then, I think of something else. *Had he meant the keys are under the tire of the car?*

Sweat rolls down my back as I scramble out of the car. The hellhound howls again, so damn close that ice runs through my veins. My hands claw into the dirt, under the driver's side tire, and then I'm crawling around the entire car, my hands digging, struggling, but there's nothing there. I want to scream in frustration, but I leap to my feet and rush back into the car, slamming the door and locking it.

Not that that will do more than slow down the beast.

I have a lot of skills, but hot wiring a car isn't one of them. Still, I'm scrambling, trying to think of anything. I reach up and pull down the visor.

And the fucking key falls into my lap.

I'm shaking, but I grab it. I try to get the key in the ignition, but I'm shaking so hard that it isn't working. My head jerks up, and I look behind me to see the hellhound, with its silver collar, just a short distance from the back of the car. Fire erupts on its back, blinding in intensity, but nothing is as intense as the scarlet fire in its eyes.

The key slides into the ignition, and I turn it. The engine roars to life, and I put it in drive, not giving a shit about the branches thrown over the car. I step on the gas and peel out of the woods, aiming for the road. The ground beneath the car is uneven, so rough that I'm pitching and rocking so hard my foot is sliding around on the gas pedal, but I don't slow.

It's chasing my car. Of course the fucker is. Its massive paws are pounding against the ground so hard that I can imagine I can feel it shaking the very earth. My gaze keeps moving from the woods in front of me to the beast behind me. When I hit the road, I almost want to cry in relief, but then he hits the road and gets even faster.

Fuck.

I push the pedal down to the ground, and the car leaps forward like a wild animal fully trying to survive this hunt. My hands are so sweaty on the wheel that it's hard to hold onto, but I do. I hold on like the smallest mistake will cost me my life, which it will. My gaze continues to move from behind me to the road ahead, and I feel overwhelmingly grateful as the beast slowly starts to fall further and further behind.

But it isn't until I turn off the small road leading to the castle and hit the larger road, leaving the hellhound completely behind, that I take my first deep breath. Okay, maybe leaving the safety of Rian's lands was a mistake. But I'd survived the damn beast. Now, I just need to reach my father and his people, convince them to stop this war, and get home in one piece.

I can do this. I think.

My entire body is shaking and sweat is rolling down my back, so I flip on the radio and try to turn on something peppy to help me forget what just happened. It doesn't work, but I force myself to sing along to the music anyway. It's something I used to do back at the academy when I needed to calm myself down, to pretend that the cruel other students weren't getting to me. The hours crawl by with song after song of pop music playing until I realize that I'm almost out of gas.

I wait until I see a sign on the side of the quiet road indicating a gas station a few miles ahead, then pull off and start pumping gas. Realizing that this will be my last stop for the night, I go inside, use the bathroom, grab a couple of sodas pumped full of caffeine, candy, and some other snacks, and pile it all on the counter. The tired guy behind the counter is watching me in a way that makes me uneasy, but then I remember that I've got a sword strapped to my back, I'm wearing all leather, and I didn't bother to shift my cloak around to cover myself up.

"Costume party," I tell him with a shrug as he continues to stare.

Relief hits him. "Yeah? Where? Maybe after work I could--"

"It's private." I grab my bagged-up snacks and drinks, thank him, and head for the door.

"Maybe I just want to know what's under those clothes," he tells me in a voice that creeps me the hell out.

I roll my eyes. "Not even in your dreams."

Outside, I shove the drinks into the passenger seat, then notice that the pump's stopped and go to take it out of the car. Which is exactly the moment a chill rolls down my spine. I'm still holding the gas filler when I slowly turn around. There, just a few feet from me, is another hellhound. It wears a silver collar, like the last one, but it's nearly twice the first hellhound's size.

I watch its back legs tense, and barely have a moment to recognize it's about to jump when I'm moving. The gas filler falls, and I dive to the side, between pumps. I hit the ground, hard, but I also hear the hellhound hit the ground where I'd been just a moment before. Rolling, I leap to my feet and race for the store. I might not make it, but somehow, I think I might have a better shot of escaping it behind a locked door than in the woods.

It growls so long and low that goosebumps rise on my skin, but I don't look back or slow. To do either would cost me my only chance at escape.

I hear its massive paws hitting the pavement behind me, too close, but then, I'm at the door, swinging it open. "Lock the door! Lock the damn door!"

The man behind the counter's mouth simply drops open in shock. I leap over the counter and hit the button under the cash register, locking the place up with one touch. The hellhound though, it doesn't give a shit. The bastard comes exploding through the glass door, sending sharp shards across the entire store. I duck, but just for a second, before I start to run again for the back, praying the door doesn't have some kind of code.

"Watch out!" the cashier screams.

This time, I glance back as I'm almost at the door, and sure as hell, the beast is just feet behind me. Bullets ring out, slamming into the hellhound, but they also whizz past him, hitting me in the stomach, and then the shoulder. I let a loud gasp as the pain moves through me, and the hellhound growls and turns around.

At that moment, I know the man is dead. At any other time, I'd try to help. But my legs feel like noodles underneath me, and my vision is shifting from too bright to black. My body seems to be begging me to pass out, but I push the feeling aside and reach clumsily for the door handle as the beast races toward the cashier.

To my relief, someone propped the door open just a little with a water jug, and I weakly kick it out of the way, then slip into the back, slamming the door behind me. My arm is wrapped around my stomach. I feel warm blood coating my clothes and my arm. I'm pretty sure I'm walking slightly tilted, but I just keep moving forward.

And then, I hear more bullets, followed by screaming and then silence. I have no doubt the hellhound simply killed the human out of irritation. I'm his target to drag back to his master.

As if it read my thoughts, I hear a massive boom against the door. Growling. Scraping. And I have no doubt within moments the beast will have broken through the door. But I just keep moving forward until I see the door that hopefully leads to the outside. I turn the handle, struggling, my vision still wavering, and come out into the night. Closing the door silently behind me, I stumble back to my car, glancing back at the gas station to see not only the broken glass painting the whole place but also blood.

I'm shaking as I slip into my seat, turn the engine on, and pull back onto the road. Glancing back once, I see the hellhound explode out into the parking lot, searching for me, but then I leave it far behind.

My focus turns to the road. I'm close to my father. To the phoenixes. Closer than I am to my men, even though I wish I could be with them right now. So, I keep my focus on the road, on letting each mile fly past. I attempt to drive and wrap my wounds, but I'm light-headed, not aware if I've done any good at all.

I don't remember most of the drive. I just remember pain. I remember telling myself to just keep breathing. To just keep going. If I die, I'll come back. If I'm just severely injured, my father can help treat my injuries when I reach him.

But then I'm outside the gate to their manor. The same place I'd been sent to by the guild so long ago that it almost seems like a dream. I'd planned to get out, slip into the building, and find my father. But as I reach for my door handle, my hand doesn't seem to want to obey. The shaking within me grows more and more intense. Black edges my vision, and then, nothing.

The world is simply gone.

13

Ares

I can't seem to get comfortable on the damned couch in Rian's room. Maybe it's the blazing fire, Bash cleaning his weapons, or all the people fluttering around Rian, making sure he's ready for the coronation that night. Whatever it is, I'm on edge. I want to just go straight to Mercy. Something about her always seems to soothe me, but I'm fully aware of how upset she is about the plan to kill all the phoenixes. Mad enough to even miss breakfast, and she loves food. So whether she's sulking in her room or asleep, I can't imagine that we'd be any good to each other right now.

"What do you think?" Rian asks us, then turns away from the mirror, his tailor standing at his side.

Bash snickers, but covers the sound up with a cough.

"Uh, nice," I manage, but Rian looks kind of ridiculous. Like he's clothed for a coronation that happened hundreds of years ago. But then, the vampires certainly like their traditions, and if this is one of them, I'm not about to say a word.

"Really?" Rian asks, lifting a brow in my direction.

I shrug.

Bash is hiding a laugh behind his hand and doing a poor job of it. I know for a fact that if the tailor and servants weren't here, he'd be laughing his ass off, but he knows better than that. People might know we're Rian's friends as well as employees, but we have to still behave in a respectful manner.

"I don't know." Rian looks back at himself in the mirror. He's wearing a large cloak. The top half is made out of some kind of white fur, and the bottom half is a velvety red material. And there are white bows on the sides of the cape. Underneath that, he's wearing a red...almost suit, but it's too frilly and decorative. It's covered in gold and jewels that just seem like too much. Oh, and then there's the massive ruby broach closing the cape over his suit.

I just have no clue what to say that isn't a lie, or completely insulting and unhelpful, but I try. "It looks traditional."

The tailor seems relieved. "Every male in the Drakkar family has worn some variation of this outfit for all their coronations. We have pictures dating back to, well, dating back as far as you can imagine."

"So then, it's perfect," I stammer out.

Rian gives me that look. The one that says he knows what I'm not saying. "If it makes my father happy, then I guess it's perfect."

The tailor helps him take off the ridiculous clothes and places them on a mannequin near the mirror. Rian thanks him for his efforts, and then asks the servants, who are fixing the sheets and blankets on his bed and setting out more food, to leave. As Rian puts on a button-up white shirt and black slacks, the servants drift out, and then we're finally left alone.

Rian collapses onto the couch beside Bash, eyeing the snacks that have been set out. "This is terrible."

Bash snorts. "That *outfit* was terrible. *This* is a tragedy."

Rian laughs. "I knew I was always going to be king, I just thought I had more time. And I imagined that when I did take the crown, I wouldn't feel like a puppet. I'd have gained my father's, and my people's, respect. But this, it's exactly what I don't want. Everyone seems to think this is perfect. That I'll be king and still be under my father's thumb, changing nothing. I want them to be wrong, but my word binds me in ways I never wanted."

Bash grabs a cookie and bites into it messily. "Listen, man, we'll go over your promises and find ways around them. Okay? For today, you just have to make a good impression on all those powerful people downstairs, remember everything you're supposed to say, and just power through the day."

"Maybe you're right," Rian says. He leans forward, glancing over at the choices. There's a plate of blood sausages, that are *really* blood sausages, and he takes the one on top.

He's about to put it in his mouth when I spot something, and my instincts take over. I launch out of my chair, and smack the sausage to the ground, breathing hard.

"What the hell?" Rian shouts.

"Something was wrong."

They both stiffen.

I climb down to the ground and pick up the sausage. It's a slightly lighter shade than the others, and when I sniff it, I know for sure something is wrong with it. "I think...I think this has been poisoned."

Maybe I'm wrong. Maybe I'm just on edge. But it doesn't matter; Bash has launched into action, calling in the guards.

They take the sausage to test it, and Bash lets everyone know what's going on, asking for an increase in guards, and the names of everyone who had been in the room.

Two hours later, we know the sausage would have killed our Rian. It was bespelled, woven with a powerful and expensive spell that would have ended his life within moments. We've also accounted for all the servants, save for a young woman, who has since disappeared. And if we all thought we were on edge before, it's nothing compared to now.

Our job is to guard Rian. We might have been kicked out of the guild, but regardless of whether we have our credentials or not, it's our primary responsibility to keep him safe. We relaxed to much at the worst possible moment. It won't happen again.

What's more, the phoenixes had attacked another great family the night before. People are whispering about it, but we still don't know much, other than that no one we are close with was injured. It isn't a good feeling though, either way.

The rest of the day isn't any easier. Rian is trying to find out the spell his father will use to hide Mercy and protect her, but no one other than his father seems to know, and the stubborn king will be sure not to tell him until after the coronation. That we all know for sure.

There are also whispers of something different having happened after the last attack with the phoenixes. Something about their numbers decreasing. But, again, they're all just rumors.

Rian sends me to slip between the important people arriving in droves. Many of them are from the twelve families, all with different stories about the attacks. Some say the phoenixes did very little of the actual fighting, leaving the other supernaturals to take the brunt of the fighting, while others describe the phoenixes like fiery creatures of vengeance.

I can't pick out the lies from the truth. So, eventually, I return to Bash and Rian, wanting to clear my head before the coronation. Wanting...I don't know what, but to feel just a little less of the tension building in my chest.

"You okay?" Bash asks me.

We're in the library with Rian, staring at our mountains of papers about the phoenixes, probably because this is something to focus on outside of the chaos in the castle. All the people. The attempt on Rian's life. The fact that after today, everything will be different. Rian will make all the decisions regarding his people. His life will be in danger on a totally different level, and in a weird way, all of us will have lost our freedom.

I nod slowly, but realize that I'm not okay. I want to fucking crawl out of my own skin. "I think I just need some air."

"Get some," Rian says, his tone a little sharp. "One of us should at least not be miserable."

"You sure?" I ask, even though I really want to go.

He waves for me to leave, so I do, making certain that the guards at the door are familiar and trusted before I do.

Everywhere I go, there are more visitors. More rich vampires. There are also representatives from the twelve families, but because of the danger and loss, most were not able to send all their family members. It's almost...in bad taste to be having the coronation with so much going on. Yet, it's not my place to question the king. He's never been the sentimental sort, more like the vengeful type, so I don't think the injuries, destruction, and losses of life means much to him. Just getting through this and finally being done with his responsibilities.

Or maybe just doing this before Rian can change his mind. Probably a little of both.

The vampires know who I am. Everyone knows who my father and I are, but it doesn't stop the dirty looks. Nor the whispering. Words like, "mutt," "dirty," and "pathetic," are spoken as people pass me. And by the time I've seen a few dozen of the vamps, I want to run from them too.

So, I hurry for the outdoors, slip into the woods, and shift. My wolf practically moans in satisfaction, and then we're racing around. Enjoying the smells. The fresh air. And the freedom to just *be*. I let my wolf take complete control, and we even end up taking a small nap in the sunlight.

When I wake up, I'm feeling better. I return to my clothes, shift back, and can't help but notice the spring in my step.

That is until I see the black van circling to the side of the manor.

With narrowed eyes, I use the cover of the woods to hide my movements and circle closer. Vampires that I know work for the king climb out of the van, and then they go to the back and throw open the door. More vampires haul out people who are bound and have bags over their heads, and drag them through a side door.

Unable to help myself, I follow them into the castle, slipping into the shadows, and using my skills from the guild to stay out of sight. I watch as they take the people down to the basement, then return to the first floor, my mind racing. I'm going to go figure out what the hell is going on, just in case whatever it is could hurt Rian, but I don't like any of it. If they were bringing in more blood slaves, they wouldn't be subtle about it.

So who are those people?

I wait for the group of vampires who came down to leave. And once I'm sure they're gone, I slip down to the basement. It's not like I'll get in trouble for being down here. The basement is mostly just not a place people want to hang out, or that guests want to go to. It's a prison for blood slaves, and the doors and locks seem to be enough to keep a bunch of weak people where they are. *Big surprise, huh?*

Yet, I only go down there to help them. Otherwise, I avoid it. Even as a young boy I hated that Rian's family kept blood slaves. My father said he didn't agree with the use of blood slaves, but that this is how things were done amongst the vampires, and we needed to respect that. I don't, but I also respect that some situations just suck, and I can only do as much as I can.

So, over the years, I have brought them food, card games, books, clothes, blankets, whatever I can manage, always reminding myself that if I try to free the slaves, they'll simply be rounded up and killed. It's not much, but it's better than nothing.

Because it's morning and most of the slaves haven't been drained yet, they're awake. After being drained, they mostly just lie on the floor, exhausted. But now, they play card games between cells. Eat their breakfasts. Read books. Whatever. It's certainly better than when we went down here with Mercy.

As I walk down the hall, there's the low murmur of voices and even laughter. They tense when they see me approaching, but then relax once more when they realize it's only me. They know if I'm here, it isn't for trouble. They also know better than to draw attention to the fact that I'm here.

Yet, I don't see anyone new.

I keep going down the main path, but everything is as it

seems. Most of the blood slaves here last for years, twenty to thirty if all goes well. The king has never been a man to overfeed and kill one, or cause unnecessary harm to them, which I'm grateful for. Rian and I have never really understood why he doesn't just get willing feeders, since he tries to treat them so well. Bash said it was a pride thing. That if the vampire king only got willing feeders, the other vampires would see him as weak, then kill him and replace him. I wish I could say that they'd never do that, but if the king seems old school, most of the other vampires are *old*-old school.

A few of them wave to me. Mike gives me his goofy grin, and Brenda looks up from the book I snuck to her the last time we were here. She's probably read it quite a few times since then, so I make a mental note to bring down more books.

Still, there's no one new. I check the whole main hall, then split off to the small hallways. These aren't all prison cells. There are supply rooms. A few...almost bedrooms, in case a vampire wants to feed down here, and some rooms that look like punishment rooms. Although they could be sex rooms for when the vamps are done feeding. I've never been brave enough to ask.

At the end of one hallway is almost a receptionist area. Or maybe like the central hub in a hospital. There's a circular desk in the middle of the room with computers, office supplies, and chairs. Then there are couches around the room. It's another area I haven't figured out, but prison cells line the outside of the circle.

Prison cells that are always empty.

Except for today.

Two women and three men are each in separate cages. Their hands are bound behind their backs. The two women are sleeping, looking in rough shape, from their dirty and stained clothes to the bruises and cuts that line their bodies. Two of the men have to be passed out. Their faces are so beaten in I'm not even sure if they can open their eyes. But one man is sitting up, his back against the wall of his cell. And there aren't any chairs, shelves, bedding, etc., to make the cells look homier. It's just an empty cell with a toilet in one corner.

When he spots me, he looks up, but his gaze is calculating. Unlike his friends, there's not a single injury that I can see, even though his clothes are soaked with dried blood and are torn in various places that look like stab and bite wounds.

"Hello," he greets me like we're two friends bumping into each other in a supermarket.

"Hi," I tell him awkwardly.

"You're not a vamp." His gaze runs over me in a way that's almost mocking.

"No, I'm not." I move closer to his cage and inhale slowly. My nose wrinkles. And, at first, all I can smell is blood. But then I pick up his natural scents and feel even more confused. He almost smells...human, but I find that hard to believe for some reason. The guards wouldn't have kept a human bound. And if he was just a blood slave, he'd be with the others. "You're not a vamp either."

"Nope." He smiles, but there's nothing nice about his smile. "I'm a phoenix, but I'm sure that's no surprise to you."

My jaw drops. *A phoenix? Here?*

"Technically, a half-breed. Half-human and half-phoenix, like most of us. But then, there are only two pure phoenixes left, so I'm not sure it even matters anymore."

I stare at him, not knowing what to say. "You're...prisoners? From the attack?"

"Smart man." His smile drips with sarcasm. "But most of us got away. Alive or dead, it doesn't matter. We'll be back, and then the killing will continue."

"For how long?"

He gives an awkward shrug with his hands bound behind his back. "We have no plans to ever stop. We're going to track down every family line that ever hurt a phoenix. We'll kill the grandparents, most of whom enslaved our parents, kill their kids, their grandkids. We'll kill their damn dogs and cats. Cut their babies to pieces. And then, when everyone's dead, I'm sure we'll find more people to kill. And with those family lines gone, we'll also take over. *Everything*. Before long, phoenixes will be running this world."

"That seems...like a bloodthirsty plan."

"We live to kill," he says, giving another awkward shrug. "It's our motto."

"Maybe your motto should be learning that you can forgive without forgetting, and then create a better, safer life for your children."

He snorts. "Solarius tells that kind of shit to the weak-minded. That if they want kids, mates, and lives, they have to kill these people or they'll never be free. But he doesn't have to pull that shit with me. I know what we are...an army for vengeance. An unstoppable force that will take life and power any way we can get it."

I stare at him. My heart aches for what the phoenixes went through. No one should ever be hurt like that. No one should ever want to escape their pain so badly that they're left with no choice but to do something drastic. But this man, and this plan, it won't bring healing. It won't bring a better life for the phoenixes.

"Solarius doesn't sound like the kind of leader that will show you a path to happiness."

"He will, when he becomes whole once more."

"Whole?" *What the hell does that mean?*

There's a glint in his eyes. "I'll tell you what. I'll give you the info you need if you release me."

"I didn't say I need any info from you." I turn around, not sure if I'll actually leave, but I don't like being around this guy. He makes my skin crawl.

"Even info about his daughter?"

I freeze and turn around, no longer feeling sick. No longer even feeling pity for this guy. Just pure and utter rage. "What the fuck are you trying to say about Mercy?"

He knows he has me. I can see it in his eyes. "She's with him now, you know. Showed up at our gates riddled with bullet holes. The kind thing to do would have been to kill her and let her come back whole. But Solarius is anything *but* kind."

"No way. Mercy is here. With us."

"Is she?" He lifts a brow, and I swear to God I'm going to tear his face off.

And then I think about last night. How angry Mercy was at the idea of all the phoenixes being killed. How she thought it'd be better to communicate with them. And the fact that we hadn't seen her yet this morning. All the puzzle pieces slowly come together in my mind until a growl rolls from my throat and my hands curl into fists.

"Where is she?"

He licks his lips, then smacks them, like he's eating something tasty. And if I had the keys to his cell, I'd go inside and beat his face in until all he could taste was blood. Then he says, "I think where she is is less important than *what* her father has planned for her. Which I'll tell you, is awful. Sick. Worse than anything I'm capable of."

If he, or anyone else, actually has our Mercy, they'll wish they could die. Not that I entirely believe this bastard. The second we're done talking, I'll run until I see her, not giving a damn if I look like a moron.

"What does her father plan to do to her?" And the words come out a growl. My claws slowly elongate, and for the first time, he looks nervous.

"Release me, and I'll tell you everything. Everything you need to save her life."

I'm about to say more when I hear a noise down the hall, talking, too loud to be the prisoners. My feet take me across the room, and then I'm ducking behind the desk in the center of the room, half-crawling underneath to hide from whoever might be coming. Somehow, I doubt the king wants anyone to know about the phoenixes being kept prisoner. He might not have me killed for this knowledge, but I can see him imprisoning me down here too, until he can execute his plan, just to be cautious. And I can't be kept down here. Not when Mercy needs me.

The voices and footsteps come closer, and I stiffen when I pick out the low timber of the king's voice. A minute later, the voices sound like they're right beside me, and I'm doing my best to calm my racing heart and breathing.

"So, this is them," the king says, a sneer in his voice. "They don't look so powerful."

An unfamiliar voice responds. "Phoenixes are unique. They're not necessarily stronger or faster than humans. They do have some unique senses, but they're essentially humans. Until, of course, they die, and then they come back with all their injuries healed. With pure-blood phoenixes, they come back faster and more powerful every time they're killed. With these half-breeds, it seems to take them some time to come back, although it varies based on their genetics. They also tend to come back healed, but sore from death. That's about all we know about them right now."

"As well as how to kill them." The king sounds more than a little pleased.

Has he really found a way to do it? No one, as far as I know, has ever found a weakness in what the phoenixes can do, but I've never exactly studied them. And if there's information out there, the king is powerful enough and wealthy enough to find it.

"Kill might not quite be the right word, but permanently stop them coming back, yes, I believe we've figured it out."

"Idiots!" the phoenix shouts. "You will never stop us. We're unstoppable. And one day, you'll all be dead, and we'll be dancing on your graves."

There's a pause. Then King Drakkar says, "Give it to me," and goosebumps rise across my flesh.

I crawl to the edge of the opening to the circular desk area and peek out. The king is there, surrounded by four of his men. One of the men hands the king a gun, and I can't help but frown. I'm pretty damn sure that people have tried shooting phoenixes before.

King Drakkar holds out the gun to the smirking phoenix and fires a shot straight into the man's chest. The phoenix stares down in shock as blood begins to pour from the wound. But before he even opens his mouth, something starts to happen. Terror awakens in the man's face as his eyes widen, and then his entire body turns to stone. His terror is frozen on his face forever, almost like a twisted statue.

"It works." The king sounds pleased.

"I told you it would." The other man gives a respectful bow, then starts to turn.

I jerk back, to stay hidden behind the desk. I hear

someone placing things on the desk, then the king speaks again. "We don't have a lot of time. I'll take one of them and a few rounds. The other stays here. And the final one you'll use to make more, enough to end the miserable lives of every last phoenix, other than my son's mate. Anyone touches her and they'll wish they could die as peacefully as the rest of the phoenixes."

Nothing more is said. Footsteps move away from the hall. But still, I remain hidden until I'm sure the king and his men have gone.

At last, I rise to my feet and see about a dozen guns lying on the table with several huge containers of bullets next to them. Without a thought, I take one of the guns and some bullets and hide them in my pockets. The phoenix might have been lying about her being taken, but either way, I'd feel safer protecting her with a weapon like this.

I'm about to leave when I look back at the phoenix one more time. I don't regret what happened to him, he was an asshole, but I wish I'd gotten more information first.

What's more, I can't stand the thought of this being the fate of all of the phoenixes.

Something needs to be done. First, Mercy. Then, the phoenixes.

I just hope the phoenix was lying and that Mercy is safely upstairs.

God help us all if she's not.

14

Rian

My heart is racing as I stand in front of the mirror in my coronation clothes. Tonight is the night. And more than anything else, I just want Mercy by my side. Yet, she's still avoiding me. Ignoring me. Not attending any meals nor coming to see me.

I spent some time reflecting this afternoon and came to the horrible realization that I was fine with this coronation. I've never been a particularly dishonest or manipulative person, and will one hundred percent follow through with my promises to my father, but I also fully believe that with Mercy by my side, I'll never cross certain lines. Lines I can never come back from.

And for the benefit of my people, I think I'll make a good ruler. My father always led with an iron fist, and although I won't be soft with my people, I believe I can rule them in a way that won't cost me my soul.

And it's because of Mercy.

She has faced impossible things. My opinion of her has

evolved and changed over time. At first, she was the woman who tried to kill me. The mysterious person I was obsessed with learning everything about. I wanted her, wanted to punish her. Teach her a lesson. *Something.*

Never did I think I wanted her heart. Or to be lucky enough to be given her heart. But that's what happened. And now, I feel different. Stronger.

What's more, she's the one woman I know should be safer at my side than away from it. No one can kill her. Anyone who might try to hurt her will have the entire vampire race hunting them day and night. And after the coronation, my father will give me the spell that will allow her to be concealed from the people who might track her. Anyone who might think they can simply send a hellhound after her and take her powers for themselves will learn otherwise.

It's perfect. *Everything* is perfect.

I've come to this weird place where, as long as I have my best friends and Mercy at my side, I fully believe I can handle anything. I'm at peace with this. Even the ridiculous outfit isn't enough to destroy the pride I feel swelling my chest. Soon, I'll be leading my people, hopefully while married to Mercy, and live a life with the people I love most around me.

There's a light knocking at the door.

"Come in!" I call.

A minute later, Bash and Ares arrive dressed in their finest: dark suits with jackets and dark ties. Both suits are tailored to perfection, made from fine material, and make them look far older and more mature than I've ever seen them before.

"You look nice," I tell them, and mean it.

They smile, and Ares says, "You look nice too. Very...kingly."

It's a stretch. I wouldn't exactly describe myself as looking nice, but at least the kingly part is right. "Is Mercy ready?"

They both stiffen. Ares avoids my gaze, but Bash answers, that careful mask of his in place, "We'll see her afterward."

"Afterward?" I frown. "She should be there. She can't possibly be angry enough not to be there."

Bash shrugs. "We'll see her after. You just need to focus on what you have to do today."

Something about this doesn't seem right, so I head for the door. "I want to see her."

Bash moves to block my path. "That's not a good idea."

"Why not?" My voice holds a threat.

"It's just not."

"Bash, what the fuck is going on?"

He hesitates, and I know he's going to lie, so I spin toward Ares. "What the fuck is going on?"

Ares reluctantly meets my gaze and then I know there's a problem.

"Speak!" I snap, then pull a card I never pull. "Tell your future king the truth. *Now*."

Ares's bright green eyes hold surprise, but he speaks. "We think she left last night to go to her father and the other phoenixes to try to convince them to stop the attacks."

My blood runs cold. "And where is she now?"

"She hasn't come back, but I've informed both my father and your father about the situation, and they've sent people to search for her."

"But they haven't found her," I say, even though I already

Mercy's Rise

know the answer. I reach for the broach keeping my cloak on my shoulders. "We need to go. Now. We need to find her, because you sure as hell bet that girl is in trouble."

"Stop." Bash's voice is a command this time, which pisses me off.

My gaze snaps to him. "*Our* fucking woman is in trouble. We're not going to some party when she needs us."

"This isn't a party. If you don't show up tonight, if you embarrass your father, he will have you killed. He'll have another heir, and forget all about you." I open my mouth to speak, but Bash interrupts before I can. "You know I'm right. And you also know that I love Mercy more than anyone in this world. If I thought you racing away from your coronation might be the thing to save her, I'd have you do it in a heartbeat and run away with all of you. But I don't think that's the case. We have a plan to bring her safely home. We'll tell you all about it when we're done. For now, you need to become king so that when we save Mercy, she has the safety of your position to protect her."

My heart races. "I love her."

"We all love her."

"If anything should happen to her..."

"None of us will ever have a moment of joy or peace again." His hands are curled into fists, and his eyes blaze.

"I believe you," I say, but my soul is aching. "But I want to have her here now. I want to know she's safe."

"We all want that. So, hurry your ass up and get this over with so we can get to her."

I pause. "Have you called Henry?"

"Henry?" Ares and Bash say together.

I nod, my thoughts swirling. "He was the best tracker. One of only a few. He should be able to find her exact location. And if his mind isn't there, Mercy left him the potion. He can use it to save her."

"I'll call him right away," Ares says, pulling out his phone.

I'm tapping my foot, knowing I'll be late soon if I don't leave, but I can't bring myself to go. Ares speaks to a variety of people before they send the call through to Henry. When he starts talking to the old tracker, it's clear he's not having a good day, but Ares convinces him to take the potion, and suddenly, the conversation changes. Ares rattles off the situation. I don't hear the response, but Ares grows quiet, thanks Henry, and gets off the phone.

"Where is she?" I ask, heart racing.

Ares shakes his head. "It doesn't make sense."

"Where?" Bash repeats.

"He could be wrong."

"Ares!" I snap.

Ares looks up at me with big eyes. "Right outside the gates of our castle. And, she's not alone."

My father is suddenly sweeping into my room, Ares's father at his side. "Time to go!"

I straighten my spine. "Mercy went to speak to the phoenixes and hasn't been seen since. A tracker just told us she's just outside of our gates, which likely means our enemies are too."

Ares's father gives my father a look. "I told you they wouldn't be able to resist the temptation of having us all in one place at once."

"What the hell does that mean?" I demand.

My father looks back at me with a smile. "First, the coronation. Then, we save your woman and our people."

"We have to go now!"

He moves toward me, grips my shoulder like he wants to tear it off, and says, "First, the coronation. Then, the spell you want so desperately to protect your woman. Then, the phoenixes. If you try to approach this in any other order, I can't promise your woman's safety."

I glare at him as my stomach aches. *I guess...I have no other choice.*

15

Mercy

My eyes flash open and my entire body hurts in a way I've never experienced before. I try to move and my head spins like I'm on a ship that's pitching wildly in a storm. There's a moment where I think I might hurl, but then the nausea passes.

Gasping in deep breaths, I glance around and realize I'm in the woods. Only the moonlight highlights the trees in its glow; everything else is dark around me. Eerily so. And yet, it's not just the woods that are around me. Dozens and dozens of people are too, speaking in low voices.

Unfamiliar people. And some of them are *right* beside me.

I force my eyes to close, taking in slow, even breaths, letting my senses stretch out. First, I realize that my body hurts like hell. Narrowing down the pain, I remember the gunshots in my shoulder and stomach. That makes sense to me. What's weird is that they don't *feel* right. Not like an injury that's been closed and cared for, nor one that has magic woven into it to help me heal faster. It's almost as if...I've been wrapped up, and that's it.

Which makes no sense.

My memories come back slowly. I remember being shot. I remember the hellhound chasing me. Then, flashes of a long drive and gates. *Gates! Shit, I'd run to my father and the phoenixes!* That must be why I don't recognize the people around me. *But why am I in darkened woods, my wounds uncared for, if I ran to people who should want to help me?* Something is wrong.

I steady my breathing, stretching out my senses further. Waiting.

And I'm rewarded for my efforts. A woman with a soft, sweet voice speaks so close to me that I'm pretty sure she can reach out and touch me, but it's clear she's speaking in a low voice to not be heard. "I don't know about this."

Another woman answers her. "It's getting out of hand." She's close too, probably next to the first woman, but her voice is lower, almost velvety.

"I thought we were trying to get free of the people who might hunt us...not whatever the hell this is," a man says, and he sounds younger. Barely a man.

"This is just revenge," the woman with the sweet voice whispers.

"Agreed," the velvety voice answers. "And I'm getting tired of the killing and the dying. But if we run, our enemies will find us. Heck, the other phoenixes might hunt us, or the hellhounds. Our hands are tied."

"I don't want to do this," the man says.

"Most of us don't, but Solarius will not bend. Not on anything," Sweet Voice says, and she sounds almost afraid. Of my father.

This isn't what I imagined. Maybe it's better in some

ways that all the phoenixes aren't bloodthirsty, but what if my father is? What if he's behind all of them? Forcing these people to fight a war they don't want to fight out of fear?

I try to push the thoughts aside, but they linger. *Still, no matter where my father stands, this is an opportunity to change the path these people are on. A chance to talk to them and stop the war and bloodshed.*

Letting my eyes open, I roll my head to look at the three people. They're surrounding me. A little distance away, I see the other people, in all directions. They're trying to stay hidden in the shadows of the trees, but not entirely good at it. I look back at the three near me, and I'm pretty sure the woman with the sweet voice is the one who has short, dark hair, a round face, and dark clothes. The one with the velvety voice has long, black hair and wears similar dark clothes. And the man is definitely barely a man. Maybe eighteen or nineteen with short blond hair, bruises on his face, and big eyes.

None of them look like killers. None of them look like they belong in an army focused on revenge.

"Hi," I say.

All of them jump and their gazes move to me. But it's fear in their eyes more than anything else.

"I'm Mercy. And I'm sorry, but I was listening to your conversation." I can almost feel the color draining from their faces. "I actually went looking for all of you to talk to you about another path. One that doesn't involve killing and war."

They hesitate, and then the woman with the long, black hair responds, leaning in and speaking in a whisper, "We can't walk away now. If we do, we've made too many enemies. They'll just hunt us down and enslave us."

They're right.

Tears burn the edges of my eyes, and I try to come up with a solution. A way that these people won't spend their lives in hiding, hunted by the people who hate them, or for their blood.

And it's like watching the sun rise; that's how powerful the idea that comes to me is. It's a solution...to everything. I'm almost angry at myself for not thinking about it sooner!

I try to lean forward, but I wince, and my head spins. Again, I fight the urge to hurl, but breathe through it, and then focus back on them. "There's another way. A spell that allows you to basically be invisible. No one will be able to track us, *any* of us."

Because Rian will be king tonight and get the spell from his father to conceal me from anyone. I know if he realizes these people are no longer a threat, he'll use the spell for them *and* me. It'll give the phoenixes a way to feel safe and stop the violence. It's the perfect solution.

"And you know this spell?" the young man says, leaning forward, hope in his eyes.

Damn it. I can practically feel their excitement, and I hate knowing that I'm about to crush it.

"I don't have it. *Yet*. But, tonight, my...partner will have the spell, and he's willing to use it on all of you. If you just stop the war and bloodshed, you'll be able to leave and be safe."

"Are you serious?" the sweet-voiced woman asks, sounding doubtful.

I nod, and wince again, before pressing forward. "Remember, I'm a phoenix too. I'm not safe either. Part of why my partner sacrificed a lot was to be able to use this spell to keep me safe, so I wouldn't just lie about it." Then, I take a risk. "But there's only so much we can do if you keep killing. You're angering some powerful people."

"And if we attack tonight," the young man says. "There's no going back."

Attack? Tonight? Who?

"We should tell the others," the woman with the long black hair says. "Tiffany, go and spread the word that there's another way."

The other woman nods and stands, then hurries off. I'm not sure how hopeful I should be, but it's something. More than I had before. It's just...so much of this isn't making sense. *Where's my dad? Why did these people leave me injured? And where are we and who are they planning to attack?*

The young man comes closer to me, kneeling down at my side. "I'm Charles."

"Nice to meet you, Charles," I tell him, trying to smile even though the movement feels like too much.

"And you're really his biological daughter and a pure phoenix?" He sounds excited.

"Pure?" I don't really like that word for some reason. "Yeah, both my parents were phoenixes, I guess, but I don't really know anything about my biological father. I don't even understand why he never seems to be around and does that...fading to ash thing."

He looks surprised. "It's because he gave a piece of his heart to Lady Ravenwood. It allowed her to live forever, unless actually killed. But it makes it so he sort of lives forever in this in-between place. He says his consciousness is always awake, always aware, but it takes a lot of time and effort for him to reform himself, to have a body, and then he can only keep that shape for so long."

Strangely, that makes sense. "And, since he escaped, he's just spent years...planning all of this?"

"From what I understand, he was locating all of us, but he didn't start talking to us until about a year ago. Then, he went to each of us and warned us about the dangers that were coming for us. Most of the phoenixes didn't believe him, until they were killed and came back. None of us can remember the first time we died, but he was there afterward, warning us that the moment we came back to life, other creatures would feel our power and come for us."

Something is bothering me about his story. "And did they?"

He nods. "Most of us lost our parents or loved ones. They were murdered because of what we are."

"By hellhounds?" I'm shocked. Most of the time hellhounds only track the person they're tasked with tracking. But like the one with me in the gas station, if someone hurts them, it's often enough for them to react out of anger, briefly, before refocusing on their victim.

He shakes his head. "No, like I came home from school a few days after Solarius warned me that I needed to leave my old life behind in order to protect the people I love." His voice cracks a little. "But I didn't listen. Didn't believe him. I remembered pieces of dying. An axe. Screaming. Pain. I saw the path through the forest where I was killed, covered and splattered in my blood. But still, I didn't know about the supernatural. I didn't know that my family line had phoenixes in it and that, for some reason, I was more powerful than others in my family had been. I just thought he was crazy. And then I came home and found my mom, sister, and father ripped apart all over my living room." He sounds on the verge of tears.

"I'm so sorry," I whisper.

He shakes his head. "He told me *they* did it. The people who track and torture my kind. And with no family, no one left, and knowing that I'd become a magnet for trouble, I went to the castle he left me directions for."

My gut is turning. None of this...seems true, and yet, I don't think he's lying. The twelve powerful families might send a hellhound to drag a phoenix to them. They might send spells or other trackers. But they wouldn't slaughter an entire human family. Nor would a hellhound. That's just not how they work.

And yet the only explanation I can come up with for what happens terrifies me. *Could my father have killed this boy's family to force Charles to join him?*

"Is that what happened with the other people here? Their loved one were murdered and they joined this group?"

He nods. "Almost all of us." He studies me. "Why? Isn't that what happened to you when you first died?"

I shake my head, then regret it as my head spins for a long moment. "No." I'm gritting my teeth to keep from moaning in pain. "That's never how it works. Phoenixes were tracked by trackers or hellhounds. Their families weren't slaughtered. That would just...be pointless, and draw attention to the supernatural world, which most supernaturals actively try to avoid."

"Well, they did it to all of us," he says, anger in his voice. "At the castle, we have protection spells to keep everyone from finding us. That's why going there kept our remaining loved ones safe."

"Are you sure? Because the powerful supernatural families would gain nothing from killing your loved ones. It'd actually work the opposite way and warn you guys that you were being hunted and make you want to go into hiding."

"What are you saying?" he asks me suspiciously.

"I'm not sure what I'm saying but I have a sickening thought that I really don't want to think about."

"What do you mean? You care about your father, right?" he asks, and some of his anger has faded.

"I think so."

"I don't really know him, but I think I'd like to."

I hesitate. "No, I don't think I do. And the more I hear from all of you, the less I do."

He looks toward the other people all around us and inches closer to me. "Some of the things he has said doesn't sound right to me either, but some of the others act like I'm stupid for having any doubts. But the thing that bothered me the most...is you."

"Me?" Now, it's my turn to be surprised.

He nods his head. "What he thinks needs to happen to you. He says it's for the greater good, but I just don't know."

"What's going to happen to me?" I ask, heart pounding. Because whatever it is, it doesn't sound good.

He bites his bottom lip and looks around again, then opens his mouth.

"She awake?" A big man is suddenly at his side, making us both jump.

"Y-Yeah," Charles manages.

"He's coming; it's time," the other man says, while two others come to join him.

Charles looks at me, mouths the word, "Sorry," then stands and walks away from me.

None of which is a good sign.

"What's happening? Is my father here?" I ask.

They reach for me, and although I've never felt weaker, I try to fight them. I try to push their hands away. But within moments, they're carrying me. And the movement alone sends a scream tearing from my lips. For a minute, I'm fighting tears, and then I clench my hands into fists and begin to struggle in their arms. It's painful. Stupid, probably. But it's dark. I don't know where they're taking me, but their grip is tight, and their expressions are cold. Almost cruel. So it feels like I need to fight them.

Suddenly, a few torches spark to light. I stop struggling, and they put me on my feet, even though my knees crumble beneath me. Two men hold me now, one under each arm, and beneath the torchlight I can see that I've only been bandaged up, and that blood has soaked the bandages, my clothes, and my skin. I can't see my wounds, but without a doubt none of this is good.

The phoenixes gather around us in a half-circle, and it's like everyone is holding their breaths. Waiting. *But for what?*

My gaze sweeps over the crowd, and sure enough, I see the people I'd been speaking to whispering to others in the crowd. There are maybe three dozen phoenixes total. Most don't look the least bit like soldiers, except one. He's huge and stands out of place from the others and he's glaring hard at me. It's...weird to see. And unsettling.

Beside us, my father suddenly materializes. I've never seen him do it before, and for one moment he actually looks like a person. His skin is tan. His eyes are bright. His hair is dark. And then he's strangely dark again, like ash. Like lava rocks.

He lifts his hands. "It's time. Time to take the head of the snake."

There are a few cheers, followed by a few not so enthusiastic cheers. It's all pretty strange. These people seem...tired and unprepared. Not at all the force I imagined was killing all the powerful families.

I know when this group attacked the guild, they had other supernaturals with them. Were they the main warriors? I'm guessing they were. But all that seems to be left now are the phoenixes themselves, and looking at the group I find it hard to imagine that they're going to be fighting tonight, or *want* to be fighting tonight. *Did most of the people working with them die in the battles over the last week? Or did they abandon all this trouble?*

"We are ready..." Then he turns to me. "Almost ready." His dark eyes feel cruel as they stare at me.

"Ready to fight again? Attack again?" I ask, probing him for information. "Hasn't there been enough death and violence?"

"Not until every last one of them are dead," he snarls.

I lift my head, pausing, glad when it doesn't swim. "And then what?"

"Then, we rule everyone, as we were meant to do."

I roll my eyes. "The only leaders who say shit like that are the villains. Are you sure you're the good guys here?"

"Those people are murders! All they deserve is death and pain!" His voice holds a cruelty that makes a shiver roll down my spine.

"A lot of their ancestors did horrible things. But the people who actually hurt phoenixes are all dead. Now, you're just going after their innocent children and grandchildren. How does that make any sense?" I place my feet on the ground and use a little strength to test if I can stand if I need to. It works, but I definitely don't feel stable.

My father moves closer to me, so our faces are inches away from each other. "You weren't there. You have no idea what it was like. Your mother and I had everything. A home. Happiness. And you...the promise of a child. Then, they stole us. They imprisoned us. They drained us of our blood each and every day. Your Lord and Lady Ravenwood. They sipped our blood in goblets while they laughed and talked, like we were animals used just for their consumption. Do you know how *desperate* your mother was to give that bitch her child? Do you know how *desperate* she was to beg me to help her kill herself? Imagine that! Imagine being that broken!"

"It's awful," I say, holding his gaze. "But has any of this made what happened *less* awful?"

He doesn't answer.

"That's what I thought. But here, you have the last of our kind, and what are you doing? Bringing them death and pain. They were living normal, happy lives until you came around. How does that make you any better than the people who hurt you and my mother?" He opens his mouth, but I rush out, "I've discovered there's a spell that will keep them hidden from the people who are searching for them, from the hellhounds. If we stop this war, we can use the spell to disappear. All of these people will be able to have normal, happy lives again."

"Lies!" he snarls.

"No--"

He spins toward the phoenixes and points at me. "See! She might be one of us by blood, but they've stolen her soul. She only has one purpose now. As a tool to finish this thing once and for all."

"And what if the spell is real? What if we can have peace and go back to normal lives?" Charles shouts over the crowd, and several people murmur in agreement.

He turns to me. "Tell us the spell, if it's real?"

I hesitate. "I don't know it yet, but I'll have it tonight."

He laughs, a maniac laugh. "See! She lies, just like the vermin who raised her! She is not my daughter, not really, she's just a tool now to use to win this war."

A tool? What the hell is he talking about? "There doesn't need to be a war!" I say.

Suddenly, my father spins and punches me. My head knocks back, and I taste blood and smell ash. When I can lift my head back, my vision dances with the shifting firelight.

"It's time," he says.

Time? My thoughts are groggy. *Time for what?*

"I am meant to be a great leader. The one to end the reigns of the other supernatural families and bring about the rule of the phoenixes. But I cannot do that until I'm made whole once more. In theory, the only thing that can restore me to my former self is the heart of a full phoenix." He turns to me. "And that's the one thing my shameful daughter can do for me."

"My heart?" My words come out slurred, and I try once more to stand on my own. I manage it, but my knees shake.

A man brings him a dagger, *my* dagger, while the man holds my other one. A plan begins to form in my head. I thought the only way a phoenix could die was to rip out their own heart, but I imagine without mine, with it beating inside my father, I'll be something like he is now, and the thought chills me to the bone. I hate that I feel weak. I hate that I let myself get in this position to begin with.

But I will *not* let this man, this man who I'll never think of as my father again, hurt me. He's clearly insane. Not just because of what he went though, if what I learned about him before was true.

He steps closer to me, and I scan the crowd. Most of the people look horrified. But they also don't look like they plan to stop this.

He lifts the dagger over his head, and I know any second he'll be slicing my chest open.

"Amatus sum!" I open my palms as both of my daggers come slamming into them. I don't hesitate. I can't, or I won't be able to do it. I just react, burrowing one of the daggers straight into my heart.

Someone is screaming, but the world fades away, as does the beating of my heart.

Then, I'm surrounded by fire. Both daggers are gripped firmly in my hands, and I'm lifting above the crowd on fiery wings. Wings that light up the entire forest.

Below me, my father screams. He grabs someone's blade as he starts to fade away, then turns to the man behind him and slices the other man's chest open. My jaw drops as my father reaches into the wound and...rips out the man's heart with his bare hands.

I try to fly down, but I don't exactly know how to work my wings. I shoot a little higher, and then start to lower myself as he stuffs the other man's heart into his own chest. It's sick. The phoenixes are screaming in terror. Some are backing away.

The ash begins to fall from my father's face, revealing a man once more, and then he smiles, a sickening smile as I drop to the ground near him.

"It worked. With a half phoenix!" He sounds shocked.

His entire body turns to flesh once more, and then he's standing naked, his hands and arms covered in blood. Only his feet remain unnatural. He notices, glares at his feet, then looks back at me. "It's not enough! Bring her to me!"

A few of the big men start pushing through the crowd, heading toward me, but I spin my blades. I feel good. Reborn. Stronger than I've ever been before. Whatever these men try now, they'll be surprised to find that I'm no longer their broken prisoner.

"You really want to kill your own daughter?" I ask, and now there's rage in my voice.

"You're only my daughter by blood," he sneers.

I smile. "Agreed. Our relationship is that and nothing

more. Which means I won't have to feel guilty when I kill you."

Four big men are trying to surround me, while my father grins. And then, a bullet rings out. One of the men in front of me looks down, and blood begins to pour from his chest. More people gasp and scream, but my father and the men don't seem to care.

Until...the man begins to turn to stone. My jaw drops open as I watch, and then the man is nothing but a statue. "What the--?"

Lights flash, torches suddenly being lit. And just outside of our circle are a bunch of people. No, not just people, mostly vampires. And now I can see that just behind them is a fence. The one surrounding Rian's castle.

The phoenixes were going to attack my men?

And then I spot Rian. He's holding a gun in his hand, as are several of the other men.

Another shot hits a man beside me. Within moments, he too turns to stone. Panic fills the air, and everything clicks.

"No!" I shout. "Don't kill them! Most of them don't want to be here! They just don't want to be tracked. We don't have to kill them. We can just do the spell on them!"

I can see it in the vampire's faces. They're not going to stop. They're here to end this war, by turning every last phoenix into stone. By exterminating my kind.

Racing forward, heart in my throat, I say, "No! No more bloodshed! No more death!"

Instead of responding, the vampires continue to advance.

I turn back to the phoenixes. "Is this what you want? What you *really* want?"

A lot of heads shake. A lot of big, frightened eyes stare back at me.

I face my men, seeking their gazes. "Please!"

And then a horrifying pain slices through me. I open my mouth, and blood pours out. Someone spins me around. My father. He's holding a dagger and grinning. He moves to strike my chest, to carve me open.

Bash is suddenly between us, gripping my father's hand that holds the dagger. They struggle over it and more gunshots echo around us, but none directly next to them, probably because no one wants to hit Bash.

"Mercy!"

I turn and Ares is rushing forward while tossing me a gun. My numb hand manages to grasp it. The world seems to slow down as I turn and watch my father and Bash struggling over the dagger. My feet feel far away as I move forward. Then, pressing the gun right to my father's temple, I pull the trigger.

His eyes widen. And like a nightmare, I watch him turn to stone. Then, the gun falls to my feet, and Bash sweeps me into his arms as I collapse.

All I can taste is blood. But I can feel my wings behind me still, like butterfly wings rather than fire, but their blazing color lights up the night.

"Please," I whisper to Bash.

He looks down at me, then turns to the vampires. "Their leader is dead. Give them the choice now."

The king is suddenly there. "They don't deserve a choice. They deserve--"

Rian interrupts. "I am the king now, and I will give them the choice. Phoenixes, you can bend a knee and swear this vengeance is over. I will pardon you for your past crimes and have the spell weaved over you so that you can't be found by your enemies. *Or*, you can fight tonight, and die tonight, *for good.*"

My head falls to the other side. Most of the phoenixes are gathered together like a herd trying to escape a pack of wolves.

"Please," I whisper to them.

All eyes turn toward me and Charles says, "Can we trust them?"

I don't hesitate. "I will be marrying the king. I will ensure this promise is kept, you have my word on that."

And, slowly, they bend a knee. *All* of them. The only ones who remain standing are those who are made of stone.

A woman comes to me, a witch who begins working on healing my knife wound. Bash gently places me on the ground and he and Ares surround me, death in their eyes, so much anger that they almost scare me. But slowly, my pain begins to fade.

Rian comes closer to the phoenixes. Two women are at his sides. They lift their hands and begin to murmur the words to a spell. I've been around witches before and I've felt the power of their magic. This feeling, however, cannot come close in comparison. It's like the unleashing of a storm. And even as the thought occurs to me, the wind picks up. Leaves float in the air, moving too slowly for any real storm, spinning around all of us. The trees bend. The sky darkens, blacking out the moon and stars.

And then, there's an explosion. Colors, painfully bright, fill the sky. They slowly rain down on all of us, and I feel it, like the changing in the weather. The air feels...cleaner. Calmer. New, in a way I can't explain.

"It's done," Rian says.

The witch who was working on me steps back, and my men help me stand. I still don't feel one hundred percent, but as I test my body, my wings spread from behind me once more, brightening the clearing even more with their light.

None of my people stand. They just stare at me. Everyone is staring at me.

"You can go," I say, my voice shaking a little. "You're free. No one will be able to track you again. As long as you don't hurt anyone else again, we'll leave you alone. And if you ever need anything, you know who I am and where to find me."

Slowly, the phoenixes stand and begin to move away from us. Then, they start to run.

But to my relief, no one chases them.

Rian is there an instant later, sweeping me into his arms. "Are you okay?"

I nod, feeling tears sting my eyes. "You saved them."

"I gave my word. A king's word means something. Even if my father preferred I handle things differently."

"You handled it perfectly," I say, pulling back.

He kisses me, then keeps his face inches from mine. "Don't ever do anything that crazy again."

I smile, even though I'm exhausted. "No promises."

Bash and Ares hug me next, and I slowly feel my wings fading away. But, I've changed...again. And I get the weird feeling that I can use my wings again, any time I want. But I can test that theory another time.

Ares offers to carry me, and I'm so tired that I accept. Then, we lead all the vampires back to the castle. The energy around us is strange though, and I fully intend on asking the guys about it. But not tonight. Tonight, I'm going to sleep.

16

Mercy

I stretch long and hard, releasing a slow sigh as I do so. The morning air is crisp and fresh. Staring out at the big lawn surrounding my castle, the trees behind that, somehow makes me feel...content. Never in my life have I imagined that I could feel happy in my own home, but I do.

And as the months have past, I've even stopped associating everything in this place with my parents. Instead, I associate it with my new life. With the three men I adore. With my brother. With Henry, who has a nurse who brings him to visit for a few hours on any day that he's up to it.

Now, every corner of this place brings new, happy memories, and it actually feels like a home. *My* home.

"Say hi!" Ares tells me, suddenly out at the balcony with me, holding out his phone.

His dad and Rian's dad are there, grinning from ear-to-ear. Both look tan and relaxed. And they're wearing matching white shirts, unbuttoned about as low as they can go. "Hi," I greet them with a grin. "How's island life?"

Rian's father actually laughs. "A lot better than leading a bunch of grumpy vampires."

Ares's father wraps an arm around the other man's shoulder. "Although, I still have one grumpy vampire to worry about." They both laugh, then kiss.

I can't seem to stop smiling. *Who would have thought that the mighty vampire king could look so relaxed?* "I'm glad. You guys deserve it."

"We definitely do! But, we have to go. We just picked some fruit and have plans for an amazing smoothie," Ares's father tells me.

We say our goodbyes, and then Ares hangs up. "I'm glad they're happy."

I pull him closer and give him a kiss. "I'm glad we're *all* happy."

He sweeps my hair back from my face, and the smile that spreads his lips makes me feel like I'm enjoying the warmth of the sun. "Anything for you, my queen."

I punch him, and he captures my hand, showing me the giant ruby ring Rian had given me on our wedding day. "I'm not a queen. I'm an assassin."

"Pretty sure you're both," he tells me with a laugh.

Bash suddenly appears at his side. "Is our assassin plotting things in the shadows again?"

I punch him on the shoulder, but he grabs my hands and drags me into his arms, kissing me so hard that my head actually spins. Then, when he releases me, I manage, "Plotting against *you*." It's not my greatest comeback, but at least I'm not just moaning in pleasure.

Rian appears beside him, his hair a little messy. "I think everything has officially been figured out."

"And does anyone suspect what we did?" I ask. We'd been going over reports all morning and calling the most powerful families to learn more about their personal experiences, even though we secretly already knew.

"I passed a law stating that no one could get new blood slaves, but that I wouldn't take away their current ones. It was agreed upon by the families without a lot of hesitation, probably because they didn't want to anger their new king."

I grin. "I wish I'd been there to see their faces."

"When the law was passed?"

"That," I say, "and when your father's blood slaves mysteriously got away...followed by the blood slaves to all the families."

He's grinning too now. "Yeah, that would've been amazing."

Ares hugs me from behind, planting a kiss on my hair. "And they saw no signs of a certain queen and her two idiots breaking anyone out."

"Not a single sign," Rian says, "and because I wasn't told anything, I could confidently say I wasn't involved."

Truly, having a half-demon, a wolf, and a phoenix taking on these missions was the perfect combination. We seemed to be able to use all our training to slip in and out of any place we wished. Working for the crown, although unofficially.

I stroke the ring on Ares's finger. The one that matched the rings on Bash's and Rian's fingers. "Ruling hasn't been nearly as boring as I had thought. Married life too."

Rian laughs and moves closer, trapping me between his and Ares huge frames. "I'm glad we haven't disappointed." And then he's kissing me too, turning my blood to fire.

When he pulls back, he lifts a brow. "Do we have time to..."

It's my turn to laugh. "Afraid not. This assassin has a job to do."

They all exchange looks, but let me go. I maneuver around them, back into the large study that we'd had redone to suit all our needs. Papers cover the table and several surfaces, but that's to be expected between the lands I have to rule and ruling the vampires. It's a lot of work, but between all of us, we manage to leave time for fun. I hadn't been joking when I'd said this was all better than I ever imagined, because it was, in all ways. And as much as my parents had said I was never suited to be a princess, I seemed to be well-suited to be an assassin queen.

I grab my cloak off of the back of a chair, pull it on, and put the hood up. As I slip out of our room, I see a couple of phoenixes approaching. Both the women are now maids in our household, and luckily hadn't been with the other phoenixes the night my household was attacked, so there's not a lot of animosity between them and my people. There had been a little in the beginning, as expected, but as more and more phoenixes arrived, and the full story of how they'd been manipulated and used came out, my good-hearted people welcomed them like family.

Checking the clock in the hall, I realize I'm a little late and speed up. I slip down one hallway, then another, before finding a shadowy corner to conceal myself in. Within seconds, I manage to steady my breathing and heartbeat.

Then, I wait.

My victim sneaks down the hallway a few minutes later, glancing into corners and peering into shadows, but he doesn't see me. I tense, ready, as he starts to walk past my hiding place. And then I leap out, grab him, and we're rolling together.

He's laughing as he whirls on me. "Again! Again!"

I cover his face in kisses, loving the excitement in my brother's eyes as we "train" to be assassins together. It's just one of many things that has changed around here. He and I have become inseparable. And although he still misses our parents, our names have become his new favorite words.

"Did she get you again, buddy?" Rian calls.

All my men are standing at the end of the hallway now. They love to watch our little games.

"Yes!" My brother grabs my cheeks, and then I lean down and kiss him as he shouts, "More! More!"

"My turn!" Bash shouts, racing toward us.

My brother shrieks and struggles out of my arms, but Bash uses his powers to appear in front of the little guy, then softly "tackles" him to the ground as my brother laughs wildly.

Ares runs toward him. "I'll save you!" He scoops my brother out of Bash's arms, but Bash grabs Ares's ankles and drags them to the ground.

Rian groans, and then he's racing toward the pile of boys, a stupid grin on his face. He dives into the pile, and then they're all softly wrestling with my brother. I sit up with my back against the hallway wall. A couple of servants see us, shake their heads with smiles, and walk past our hallway.

But I just stare at the people who have stolen my heart. Once upon a time, I felt like I was living in someone else's fairy tale, but my nightmare. Now though, this is most certainly my fairy tale. And my happily ever after too.

We're a mess, but I wouldn't want it any other way.

IF YOU ENJOYED THIS SERIES, **then grab a copy of Reaper Hospital: Code Possessive Boss to enjoy another strong heroine and her sexy guys.**

ALSO BY LACEY CARTER ANDERSEN

Stolen by Shadow Beasts

Shifters' Fae Captive

Shifters' Secret Sin

Shifters' Lost Queen

Their Reaper

Unlikely Reaper

Reaper Hospital: Code Possessive Boss

Reaper Hospital: Code Hot Nurse

Reaper Hospital: Code Stubborn Doctor

Guild of Assassins

Mercy's End

Mercy's Revenge

Mercy's Fall

Mercy's Rise

Revenge of the Blood Pack

Shifter Crimes

Monsters and Gargoyles

Medusa's Destiny *audiobook*

Keto's Tale

Celaeno's Fate

Cerberus Unleashed

Lamia's Blood

Shade's Secret

Hecate's Spell

Empusa's Hunger

Shorts: Forbidden Shifter

Shorts: Gorgon's Mates

Shorts: Harpy Rising

Dark Supernaturals

Wraith Captive

Marked Immortals

Chosen Warriors

Dark Supernaturals: Box Set

Wicked Reform School/House of Berserkers

Untamed: Wicked Reform School

Unknown: House of Berserkers

Unstable: House of Berserkers

House of Berserkers: Box Set

Royal Fae Academy

Revere (Prequel)

Ravage

Ruin

Reign

Dark Fae Queen: Box Set

Legacy of Blood and Magic

Dragon Shadows

Dragon Memories

Court of Magic (PNR World)

Chosen by Blood

Immortal Hunters

Van Helsing Rising

Van Helsing Damned

Van Helsing Saved

A Supernatural Midlife

The Ghost Hunter

The Shifter Hunter

Magical Midlife in Mystic Hollow

Karma's Spell

Karma's Shift

Karma's Spirit

Karma's Stake

An Immortal Midlife

Fatal Forty

Fighting Forty

Finishing Forty

Shifting Into Midlife

Pack Bunco Night

Legends Unleashed

Don't Say My Name

Don't Cross My Path

Don't Touch My Men

Her Demon Lovers

Secret Monsters

Unchained Magic

Dark Powers

Mate to the Demon Kings: Box Set

An Angel and Her Demons

Supernatural Lies

Immortal Truths

Lover's Wrath

Fallen Angel Reclaimed: Box Set

The Firehouse Feline

Feline the Heat

Feline the Flames

Feline the Burn

Feline the Pressure

God Fire Reform School

Magic for Dummies

Myths for Half-Wits

Mayhem for Suckers

God Fire Academy: Box Set

An Icelius Reverse Harem

Her Alien Lovers

Her Alien Abductors

Her Alien Barbarians

Her Alien Mates

Collection: Her Alien Romance

Steamy Tales of Warriors and Rebels

Gladiators

The Dragon Shifters' Last Hope

Stolen by Her Harem

Claimed by Her Harem

Treasured by Her Harem

Collection: Magic in her Harem

Harem of the Shifter Queen

Sultry Fire

Sinful Ice

Saucy Mist

Collection: Power in her Kiss

Standalones

Goddess of Love (Blood Moon Rising Shared World)

Falling for My Bosses

Beauty with a Bite

Shifters and Alphas

Collections

Monsters, Gods, Witches, Oh My!

ABOUT THE AUTHOR

Lacey Carter Andersen is a USA Today bestselling author who loves reading, writing, and drinking excessive amounts of coffee. She spends her days taking care of her husband, three kids, and three cats. But at night, everything changes! Her imagination runs wild with strong-willed characters, unique worlds, and exciting plots that she enthusiastically puts into stories.

Lacey has dozens of tales: science fiction romances, paranormal romances, short romances, reverse harem romances, and more. So, please feel free to dive into any of her worlds; she loves to have the company!

And you're welcome to reach out to her; she really enjoys hearing from her readers.

You can find her at:

Email: laceycarterandersen@gmail.com

Mailing List:

https://www.subscribepage.com/laceycarterandersen

Website: https://laceycarterandersen.net/

Facebook Page: https://www.facebook.com/authorlaceycarterandersen

Made in the USA
Columbia, SC
14 May 2022